HANNAH'S BRAVE YEAR

HANNAH'S
BRAVE YEAR

by Rhoda Wooldridge

INDEPENDENCE PRESS
Drawer HH, Independence, Missouri 64055

HANNAH'S BRAVE YEAR

CHAPTER I

HANNAH STOOD in the middle of the kitchen, the reed broom gripped in her hand. She stiffened her back, pounded the broom on the puncheon floor and stamped her foot.

"We can do it and we will! We can do it and we will!" She thrust out her chin, set her lips and stamped again. "We can do it and we will!"

"We'll do what?"

Startled, she jumped and turned. Nat stood in the doorway grinning. Under his arm he clutched a roll of quilts and on his back he carried a feather bed.

Oh dear! One more thing for Nat to tease her about. She blushed and snapped back at him to cover her embarrassment.

"What's that you've got, and why aren't you in the field helping Joel?"

"What does it look like?"

"A feather bed. Where did it come from?"

"Mrs. Cambright sent her colored boy Abednego with it. Here are some quilts, too. She said she thought you could use them."

"That was kind of her. We can use them all right. I haven't had anything on Ma's bed since"—Hannah gulped—"since we burned her feather mattress."

"Abednego wouldn't come to the cabin. He brought it out to the field. He says cholera is a ha'nt that reaches out from nowhere and grabs you."

"I'm not sure but that I could almost agree with him. Put the mattress in the other room on Ma's bedstead."

Nat dropped the feather mattress on the cords of the hand-carved cherry bedstead and looked around.

"Now what is it that you were telling the walls we could do?"

"We can stay right here, and I am going to tell every last person who comes today. We can stay here, Nat."

"And eat your burnt bacon?"

"And eat my burnt bacon. Here, help me fluff this mattress and I will make up the bed right now. Careful, now, don't wake little Angie."

Nat helped her shake and fluff the mattress, then started back to the field. At the door he called back over his shoulder, "Don't stamp the house down. We won't have any place to stay if you do."

Hannah put away the broom, wrapped the flannel holder around the iron handle, lifted the little sliding door at the back of the iron, filled it with coals from the fireplace and started ironing her blue calico dress. If she hurried she might get it ironed as well as Marty's red calico before little Angie woke. With Marty's help she had washed all the clothes and cleaned the cabin from top to bottom the day before. It had been a long, hard day's work with little Angie fretting most of the time. Poor little tyke, she missed Ma the same as the rest of them did, and the cow's milk that she had put her on when Ma got sick still didn't agree with her. Joel had offered to do without Nat in the field so that he could help her but Hannah wouldn't hear of it. Ma would not have kept a boy out of the field in the busy season and neither would she.

Never in her life had she been so tired from a day's work, and Hannah had been used to work all her life. Except for the burning of infected bedding and necessary washing, little had been done in the cabin since before Ma and Pa and little Sammie took down with the cholera.

Hannah had been in too much of a daze to see or care. Then on Tuesday Mrs. Cambright had sent word that the neighbors were all coming in on Thursday to see what they could do for them. Mrs. Cambright lived in a two-story brick house on the Santa Fe Trail and her husband kept a store in Sibley. Never would it be said that Mrs. Cambright, or anyone else, found Ma's floors unscrubbed and her children dirty. When the last piece was washed, the floors, the pine table and the split-bottomed chairs all scrubbed, Ma's loom and spinning wheel dusted and pushed back out of the way and Ma's cherry chest and bedstead rubbed until they shone, Hannah had been so tired she thought she couldn't cook a bite. Then she remembered what Ma had said: That a woman shouldn't get so tired that she couldn't give a man a square meal and a smile when he came in at night.

So Hannah had stirred up the fire and put hominy in the kettle. Then she had combed her long black hair and plaited it, brushed out Marty's tangled curls and had her wash her face and Jack's. When Joel and Nat came in she had had steaming bowls of hominy on the freshly scrubbed table along with a rasher of bacon and a pan of corn bread.

Hannah had eaten only a few bites, though. Little

Angie had waked from a cat nap and started wailing. She lifted the baby from her cradle and sat down in the rocker that Ma had used to rock them all and tried to sing to the fretting child but the words wouldn't come, only big lumps in her throat.

When the dishes were cleared away and the hearth swept and Joel and Nat had taken Jack up to the loft to bed with them, Hannah had dropped down on the bed beside Marty and thought that she could never rise again. But she did. She had scarcely dropped off when little Angie cried out. Reaching out, Hannah rocked the cradle but little Angie had cried louder and louder. Hannah got up, lighted a candle, made a sugar bit and took it to the baby. This satisfied her for a while but all night long Hannah had been up and down warming milk, rocking little Angie.

It seemed to Hannah that she had barely dropped off when Joel called her. Stiffly she moved her arms and legs, dropped back again in the soft feathers. She just couldn't get up. Then she remembered. She had to get up. There was no Ma, no Pa. She had to get up and get breakfast. She drew herself up in bed, eased her feet to the floor, started to rise and dropped back down again on the bed and wept. Tears streamed down her face and soaked the flax-linen cover of the pillow.

Joel came in with a bucket of water, set it on the

corner table and came into the bedroom and stood by the bed.

"I know," he said, bending down and resting his big hand on her head. "You feel just like I have felt every morning going to the field without Pa. Besides, you are carrying too much of a load for a twelve-year-old girl."

The sorrow in Joel's voice brought her sobs to an end. She sat up, brushed her hair out of her eyes.

"I reckon it's no worse on me than it is on you, and it's a heap worse on the little ones." She reached for her shift and her homespun dress. "Call Nat and I'll put the coffee on."

Joel went to the foot of the ladder and called Nat, then went out for an armload of wood. When he returned Hannah was patting out corn cakes in the spider over the coals. When the bacon was almost done, she went to call Marty and Jack, but one look at Marty's pale little face changed her mind. She would let her rest a bit longer. Marty had had the cholera and pulled through it but she still looked peaked. Might as well let Jack sleep, too. He cried mornings and evenings for Ma and Pa and Sammie. She smelled the bacon burning and went to pull it off the fire.

Nat came downstairs so quietly that it startled her. This wasn't like Nat. Usually he was down the ladder in two leaps, shouting at everyone and calling to Zip, his coon dog. He slumped into his chair across from Joel, his red hair, so much like Pa's, standing straight up.

Hannah set the coffeepot on the table and stared at him. "Nat Harelson, you know Ma never allowed one of us to come to the table without washing."

Nat scowled, started to answer, then stopped, got up and went to the washstand by the door. He was tall for fourteen, only a half head under Joel and, like Joel, he was square built. Hardy woodsmen, Pa had called them. Unlike Joel, Nat usually was talkative, and always he had teased Hannah unmercifully. As far back as she could remember, Hannah had been glad to see him leave the house and sorry to see him return. Ma had sometimes laughed at her complaints about him.

"Give him time. He will grow up someday all of a sudden. He is like your pa and there isn't a better man on earth to live with than your pa."

Nat loved the woods and at the slightest excuse he would drop his hoe and strike out with the gun. He kept the table supplied with meat and saved Pa time so Pa didn't complain.

When she set the burnt bacon on the table, Hannah had expected Nat to say something about it but he didn't. He just ate silently and followed Joel out the door toward the field.

"Leave the field in time to clean up a little before

noon," Hannah reminded them. "The neighbors are coming in and bringing dinner, remember."

"Reckon they think they will make up for what they didn't do when Ma and Pa and Sammie died," Nat grumbled.

Hannah's eyes filled. "Oh, Nat, they couldn't come. You know how cholera spreads. Everybody was afraid, and most of them had their own hands full."

CHAPTER II

As she started the round of housework, that awful week—when first Sammie, then Pa and at last Ma had taken down with cholera—flashed through Hannah's mind. With Joel and Nat at her beck and call, Hannah had worked day and night doing everything for them that she had ever heard of. She rubbed them with turpentine, applied hot flannels and mustard plasters and dosed them with Dr. Sappington's anti-fever pills that Joel had brought from Cambright's general store. Joel hadn't taken off his clothes the whole of that week and Nat had worked almost as hard. It was Nat who had kept Jack away from the house. He had made a little teepee from an old buffalo hide and set it at the edge of the clearing so that Jack could play Indian night and day. It was a solemn-faced, sober-eyed Nat that Hannah had never known before.

When it was all over, Joel and their Indian friend Sagameeshee dug the two larger graves beside the little one for Sammie on the north end of the farm near the river bluff. Hannah had thought that they should take them over to the Six Mile Cemetery by the little log church but Joel had said that as much as Pa loved his farm he ought to stay on it. When the last shovel of dirt was spread over the graves, Nat, with Zip at his heels, had disappeared into the woods and they hadn't seen him for two days.

They had gone back to the cabin then, just she and Joel. Jack had been left to watch the baby and Marty who was past the fever stage but too weak to be out of bed. They had walked slowly back to the cabin, the home Ma had loved so well. It was a good two-room cabin with a fireplace at each end and a loft above.

"I'll never move you again, Melissa," Pa had said to Ma that spring that they had come here from the Boone's Lick country. "And I'll build you a good home." And he had. He had used oak for the sills and hewn walnut logs for the walls. The corners were trimly lock-notched and the chimney nicely squared. But Ma wasn't there to love it any more.

"I think we had better burn the bedding they used," said Joel, gathering up the feather mattress that Ma and Pa had slept on ever since Hannah could remember. "I'll help you wash and boil the clothes and then we will whitewash the cabin inside and out."

Hannah gulped, bit back the tears and set to work.

Jack followed them around as they worked. "Where's Ma? Where's Pa?" His blue eyes were big and searching. "I want to play with Sammie," he whimpered.

Joel rested his hand on the child's head. "Jack, there are things that none of us understand. Somehow I reckon God thought it best to have Ma and Pa and Sammie come live with Him."

"But I don't want them to live with God," Jack wailed. "I want them to live with me."

The baby in her cradle woke and gave a startled cry. Hannah lifted Angie into her arms and buried her face in the baby's soft warm body. Joel sat down in a hickory split-bottom chair and took Jack on his knee while Marty, old enough to understand and young enough to feel helpless, sobbed quietly in her bed.

Hannah warmed some milk in a saucepan and poured it into a bottle that Alice Blackburn, who had just weaned a bottle baby, had sent. She gave it to the baby and then lay down on the bed with her arm around Marty. Marty was four years younger than Hannah and small for her years. Ever since Hannah could remember she had looked after Marty.

"Don't cry, Marty. I'll look after you. You are my little sister same as little Angie." She drew Marty close to her and sank from exhaustion into a deep sleep.

She awoke to the sound of little Angie's furious screams. The moon was shining in at the window, making the room as bright as day. Wearily Hannah dragged herself out of bed, went into the kitchen and filled a bottle with milk and gave it to the baby. Little Angie sucked at the nipple greedily. She drained the bottle and acted as if she were going right off to sleep but Hannah had no more than settled herself beside Marty when the baby cried out in pain.

"O-o-h, she has the colic," Hannah said dragging herself to her feet. "That cow's milk doesn't agree with her. What shall I do?"

She lifted the baby from the cradle and patted her gently but little Angie screamed louder.

"There, there, little Angie. Sister will do something for you."

She settled the baby in the cradle once more, went to the medicine cabinet over the washstand, took out the bottle of paregoric and counted out ten drops in a little sweetened water as she had seen Ma do and gave it to the baby. Presently the baby dropped off to sleep.

Somehow a whole week had passed since that lonely

night. It had been eight days now since Sagameeshee had helped to lay Ma and Pa and Sammie to rest, and the danger of cholera had passed. At the end of the second day, Nat had come in with a brace of prairie chickens, two squirrels and a rabbit. Usually so full of talk about what he had seen in the woods, Nat was strangely silent.

After a few days the neighbors started coming to the door, bringing food and offers of help along with the news. The Harelsons hadn't been alone in their suffering. Nearly half the families in the Six Mile neighborhood had been hit and many of them had suffered the loss of one or more members. The Matthews, who had come to the Six Mile Territory with the Harelsons and settled at Blue Mills, had lost their eldest son Walter, who was Joel's age. Joel and Walter had planned to go up the river shortly with the French fur trader, Pierre Roubeau. The Newtons had buried their youngest girl. A family in Sibley had lost two children. Several elderly people and small babies had died. Skip and Maggie Hopkins had lost all three of their children. Now that the word had got around that the Harelsons had been left orphans, all the neighbors were coming today and Hannah must have fresh dresses for herself and Marty and an ironed waist for Jack. Yesterday's hard work had exhausted her body but had somehow eased the pain in her heart a little.

Right after breakfast Hannah had sent Jack and

Marty to the woods to look for early blackberries. The neighbors would bring food a-plenty but Hannah wanted to add something of their own to the dinner. The first berries of the season along with Betsey's thick cream would be a real treat.

Hannah had hoped she might finish the ironing before little Angie woke but there was no such luck. She just couldn't get more than half through any piece of work without the baby's waking and crying. Most of the time little Angie couldn't keep down the cow's milk and Ma said that a baby couldn't sleep on an empty or aching stomach. Consequently, the past week Hannah or Marty had walked the floor with her.

Hannah left the iron and went to the cradle. "You naughty little girl, you kept me up half the night and now you won't let me work."

The baby stopped crying for a moment, looked at Hannah, primped her mouth and started again.

"There, there." Hannah lifted the child from the cradle, crooned softly. "Hannah isn't mad at little Angie. Hannah's going to give her a bath and a bottle." Hannah looked at the baby's gold ringlets, her wide blue eyes. "You are a beauty," she said softly, "and I love you to death."

Indeed she did love her, but Hannah wished to heaven that the cow's milk would agree with her. She looked at the walnut clock on the mantel. Good gracious! Neighbors would start coming in before long, find her in this old linsey dress and the baby not bathed.

She bathed the baby and put a fresh wrapper on her, but little Angie refused the bottle and cried even though Hannah rocked her and sang to her.

Jack and Marty came in, their pails brimming with berries.

"We found a great big patch," Jack shouted, his little snub nose, freckled face beaming with delight.

"See how big and sweet they are, Hannah," said Marty.

"They are luscious. Pa always said this land grew everything bigger."

"Hannah," Marty came over to stand by her sister. "Hannah, we—we can stay here, can't we?"

Hannah, looking into Marty's pale little heart-shaped face, felt a lump in her throat.

"I hope so, Marty. I know we could manage for ourselves. I reckon, though, it will all depend on Joel."

Pa had promised Joel that when he was eighteen he could go up the Missouri with Pierre Roubeau, the French fur trader. For months Joel and his friend Walter Matthews had talked of nothing else. Pa had known Pierre Roubeau for years. He had liked and trusted him. Last spring, when Pierre Roubeau came back down the river on his way to St. Louis, he and

Pa and Joel had talked it over and Pa had agreed for Joel to go.

Hannah put the baby in Marty's arms. "Take care of her while I change my dress, then I will hold her while you dress. Here, Jack, put on this clean waist."

Hannah went into the other room to brush her hair and change her dress. Her hair was not curly like Marty's but it was heavy; unbound, it hung to her waist. Her eyes, set far apart under a wide brow, were deep blue. She was taller than the average girl of her age and like Ma she had a look of staunchness but no excess weight.

Marty came to the bedroom door with the baby in her arms. "Hannah—Hannah," Marty's lips trembled and the tears rolled out of her dark eyes. "Will they separate us? Like Annie and Jeff and Kate Wilson when their ma died?"

"If I have anything to say about it, Marty, we will stay right here."

CHAPTER III

THEY HAD no more than changed their dresses before the first visitors arrived. George and Alice Blackburn and their four children from across the creek came in bringing a big basket of food. Alice took Marty and Hannah in her arms, patted Jack's head.

"I am sorry we couldn't come sooner, Hannah. Oh, that baby!" she exclaimed. "She is a beauty."

"Thank you. We think she is," Hannah said proudly.

"Are the boys in the cornfield?" George asked.

"Yes, they are plowing today."

"Well, I brought my hoe and axe. We all figured

to help you catch up. We are mighty sorry about your folks, Hannah, and we want to help all we can."

"We shore do."

They turned to see Amos Biddle in the door with his wife Mollie and a pack of dirty children behind him.

"Yes, sir," said Amos as he chewed a wad of tobacco leisurely. "That's jest what we wuz all aimin' to do." He came in, his family trailing him. He crossed over to the fireplace and spit, missed the fireplace and hit the hearth.

Hannah clenched her lips. Ma had had her opinion of men who spit on the floor, especially Amos Biddle.

The Biddles were followed by the Browns and the Newtons, the Powells from Sibley and the Moores from over on the Santa Fe Trail. Mrs. Cambright came in with a hamper of food. Hannah thought she looked very pretty in her checked gingham dress and matching bonnet. Mr. Cambright, she said, would leave the store with his clerk, Ephraim Locke, and come over at noon.

To be sure Grandma Peabody was there. No Six Mile neighborhood gathering was complete without Grandma Peabody. She had no children or grandchildren, only a nephew, but she was Grandma to everyone. She lived in a snug little cabin at the edge of Sibley, just close enough to town to keep track of everybody, she said. She had a garden, a few chickens, a cow and a horse, all of which she took care of efficiently. She was short and plump and round-faced, with sharp brown eyes, a quick smile and black hair almost untouched by gray in spite of her sixty-nine years. She got off her horse and walked in briskly carrying a basket. She set the basket on the table and took Marty and Hannah in her arms in one sweep.

"I would have come sooner if I could have."

They all knew that her nephew Hezekiah Williams' family had been down with the cholera but had pulled through with her nursing. She took off her black slat bonnet, tied on an apron and took charge of things.

"Too many for the house. We will have to eat outdoors."

By mid-morning the cabin was full of women and the clearing full of children. Every man had brought farm tools and they all set to work hoeing, plowing, or chopping wood. All the women took on over Angie until Hannah swelled with pride.

"I do know she is the prettiest baby I ever laid eyes on," declared Lizzie Brown. "And I've had five."

But no one could come up with a solution for feeding her.

"Most of them will do well on cow's milk," said Mary Powell, "but there is one occasionally that won't. Have you tried half milk and half water?"

Hannah said that she had tried everything she had

heard of but nothing satisfied Angie or agreed with her. "And she was such a good baby before—and so healthy."

Angie, getting so much attention, smiled and cooed for a while but presently she remembered her little stomach. She opened her mouth and screamed and no one could pacify her.

Before noon Skip and Maggie Hopkins came. Maggie looked pale and thin and sad, and Skip's usually happy-go-lucky face was sober.

"We reckoned other people have had just as much trouble as we have and we decided we'd come and see what we could do."

All the women turned to them sympathetically. To have lost all their children! What could be worse? The Hopkins were not the most respected people of the community. Skip was what Pa called an itchy-footed man, always pulling up stakes and moving from one place to another and Maggie was an indifferent housewife. But now that the Hopkins had met with tragedy, all the women wanted to make them feel that they were one of them.

"Come in, Maggie," said Mrs. Cambright, drawing out a chair. "We are so glad that you have come. You will find the men out on the place, Skip."

Everyone in the neighborhood looked up to the Alfred Cambrights, but here was Mrs. Cambright treating Maggie as if they were old friends!

Maggie passed by the chair that Mrs. Cambright drew out for her and went straight to the cradle that Hannah was rocking. "How old is she?"

"Six months."

"Same age as my little Dulcie. How is she doing on cow's milk?"

"Not very well."

Little Angie opened her eyes wide, looked up at Hannah and gave a complaining wail. Maggie lifted the baby from the cradle, sat down in Ma's rocker, unbuttoned the front of her dress and pressed Angie's downy little head to her breast. Little Angie nursed greedily making little contented sounds of pleasure. As soon as her little stomach was full, she dropped her head on Maggie's arm and was sound asleep. Hannah offered to put her back in the cradle but Maggie shook her head.

Dinner, spread under the trees, was a bountiful occasion. Everyone had brought well-filled baskets except the Biddles, who were generally accepted as community moochers and the Hopkins, who had to ride too far to carry a basket and were too sad, anyway, to put out the effort. They all smiled a little when they saw the contents of Cassie Overton's basket. Cassie had brought something, but it was mostly corn bread and hominy and a stew of rabbits too tough to fry. Cassie was as close as the bark on a tree.

There was fried young rabbit and squirrel, parsnips and turnips left over from last winter's store, wild spring greens cooked with hog's jowl, possum smothered in a nest of sweet potatoes, molasses cakes and custards. Mrs. Cambright had brought a plump hen and dumplings along with an assortment of pickles and jelly. They all exclaimed over the blackberries in old Betsey's thick cream.

"I didn't know blackberries were out yet."

"Where did you find them?"

"They are unusually early and so big!"

It made Marty smile and Hannah felt better than she had at any time lately to see Marty's little face light up.

When everything was ready, Hannah beat on the wash kettle with a hammer to call the men from the field. After everyone was helped, the men settled themselves comfortably in the shade. Jack, of course, ate with the children, but Hannah, now that she was taking Ma's place, sat with the women and Marty came around and sat beside her.

After they had eaten they talked. Mr. Cambright started it off by asking Joel if he had any plans.

Never given to words, Joel shook his head. After a moment he said, "I've been trying to think."

"Just as well," nodded Mr. Cambright. "A quick decision made at a time like this is seldom good."

"Weren't you planning to go up the river with that French trapper?" Dave Powell asked.

Joel nodded. "That was the plan. Walter Matthews and I had planned to go with Pierre Roubeau. Now Walt's gone and—everything here is changed."

"How soon had you planned to go?" Mr. Cambright asked.

"When Roubeau passed through here in April on his way back to St. Louis he said he planned to leave Independence not later than mid-July."

"Well, that gives you about six weeks. By that time you should know what you want to do."

"I can't see that there is but one thing to do," Gideon Baxter spoke up. He had ridden up right at noon. He didn't come in time to help with the work, but he had come in time to eat. Unlike the other men he hadn't come in work clothes. He wore an old frock coat that hung loosely on his long, lanky frame and a shirt with a collar that reached to his ears. "You can't leave a bunch of kids to shift for themselves."

"Now tha's jest what I was a-thinking," said Amos Biddle biting off a hunk of tobacco. "Goin' to split 'em up, might as well do it right now. Take me, I'm long on girls and short on boys. I could use a boy Nat's age."

"Looks to me like you've got about all you can house and feed right now, Amos," said Mordecai Brown.

"Well, now we would be glad to take Hannah,"

said Cassie Overton, "seeing as how her ma has trained her to work so well."

"Yes," thought Hannah, "most of them might be glad enough to take Nat and me. We are big for our age and know how to work. But what about the little ones?" She moved closer to Marty and put her arm around her shoulder.

Little Angie, who had been sleeping soundly, woke and started to cry. Hannah went into the cabin and brought her out and put her in Maggie's outstretched arms. Maggie put the child to her breast and little Angie snuggled down happily.

"I think Skip and me might take the baby home with us," said Maggie.

Hannah looked doubtful. But Mrs. Cambright nodded at her and the other women who had stayed out of the discussion until this point all seemed agreed on that arrangement.

"I think it would be the best thing for the baby," Mary Powell said.

"It would be a big help to Hannah, too. Taking care of a baby is almost a full-time job for one person."

"I think it would be a good thing for Maggie," said kind Lizzie Brown.

"Divide 'em all up," said Gideon Baxter. "And the sooner the better."

"I'm just like Mr. Baxter," said Cassie. "The sooner the better."

Marty gave a moaning sob and hid her face in Hannah's skirt.

Hannah, her face scarlet, threw both arms around Marty and turned on Cassie. "No! No! You are not going to separate us. We are going to stay here, I tell you! We are going to stay!"

Mrs. Cambright came to stand by them and Grandma Peabody took over Gideon Baxter.

"Shame on you, Gideon Baxter, for stirring up a thing like this so soon."

"Nothing to be gained by waiting," Gideon protested.

Several of the men looked doubtful and Mordecai Brown said he thought no one should rush into the matter.

"I think it is up to Joel," said Mr. Cambright.

Gideon Baxter snorted. "An eighteen-year-old boy ain't capable of making decisions."

"I was fifteen," said Mr. Cambright, "when I took over my father's farm and helped my mother to bring up six younger ones. I managed well enough and I think Joel is capable of making his own decisions."

"Thank you, Mr. Cambright. I think I am, too."

"In that case," said Mr. Cambright, "I think the thing to do is to finish our day's work and go home. In two or three weeks, those of us who are interested can come back to see how they are making out and what they want to do."

With that, the men, except for Gideon Baxter, returned to the fields and the women started clearing up the dishes.

Later, the women sat about the cabin knitting, mending and talking. Maggie Hopkins just couldn't keep her hands off little Angie. She sat in Ma's rocker the whole afternoon rocking the baby, a wistful look on her face.

"I think it might be well to let Maggie take the baby for a while," Mrs. Cambright urged Hannah before she left. "That will be a real help to you, give you a chance to get things in hand."

Joel agreed with Mrs. Cambright that Hannah had enough to cope with and if Maggie wanted the baby for a while it might be best for all concerned. So Skip and Maggie went off smiling with little Angie.

Hannah watched as they started off. "If they just didn't live so far back in the woods. If they were close by where we could see her once in a while I wouldn't mind so much."

"They will be good to her, Hannah," Joel said. "It will help you out and be good for them."

"I reckon it will," Hannah said tearfully.

The last horse was no more than out of sight when Sagameeshee appeared out of the woods. Like all Osage men he was tall and well built. The local Osage wore few clothes in summer, only a breech cloth and no ornaments. Pa said that the Osage around Sibley were poor Indians. The Osage down in Arkansas were better off. All the Osage had stone faces and cold eyes. Pa said that if other people had been mistreated all their lives like the Indians their faces would freeze, too. Many of the settlers were not good to the Osage but Pa liked most of them, especially Sagameeshee. And Ma had befriended his pretty little squaw, Pokaleeta, sending her gifts of food and beads and trinkets in exchange for the herbs and roots for medicine that Sagameeshee brought.

"Hello, Sagameeshee," Joel called.

Sagameeshee walked into the kitchen without invitation as was Indian habit.

Hurriedly Hannah filled a plate with food left over from dinner. None of the women except Cassie Overton would take a bit of the food they had brought. Although Hannah drew out a chair for him, Sagameeshee took the plate silently and went outside where he could sit with his back against an oak tree.

Hannah sent Jack to the springhouse for milk and poured out big mugs full for Sagameeshee and Joel and Nat. Indians loved milk. He spoke not a word, eating with his fingers and drinking the milk in big gulps. After he had finished eating, Sagameeshee filled his pipe, lighted it and spoke. He talked mostly in English, but at times when he was unable to express his meaning, he would use a few Osage words. Pa could understand the Osage language and Nat and Joel had picked up quite a bit of it.

"Stay here," Sagameeshee said pointing to the ground. "All stay."

"We hope to, Sagameeshee."

"Land good. Land be kind to my white brother's children. Long white man—" he hesitated, couldn't find the word he wanted. Then in Osage he said, *"mon-chap-che-mani"*—the one who crawls in the grass.

Knowing that he meant Gideon Baxter they all laughed.

With no further word he walked toward the woods.

"He probably knows what he is talking about," said Joel.

"Most Indians do," said Nat.

CHAPTER IV

AFTER SUPPER Hannah sent Marty to bed, then washed the dishes by herself, undressed and lay down beside her. Sleep didn't come immediately. For a long while she lay thinking. If Joel went West she didn't know what would become of the rest of them. Most families had all the children they wanted. She and Nat would probably go to some family like the Biddles or Overtons who wanted someone to work for free. The Hopkins, no doubt, would want to keep little Angie but what about Jack and Marty? She turned her head into her pillow and wept.

The sun was coming up with a shaft of warm light

when Hannah woke. Nothing seems so bad on a fair morning as it has the night before. Hannah dressed, combed her hair and went to the door to look out over the meadow. Pa had said it was the prettiest meadow in the world. He had been proud of his farm, said that he wouldn't trade it for any that he knew. It was a beautiful meadow and a good farm. She turned from the door, started the fire and poured hominy grits into the cooking pot. By the time Joel came in from milking, she had the coffee made and the bacon in the iron skillet.

"You ought to call Nat to help with the chores, Joel. You could get in the field earlier if you did."

"I reckon we could but Nat's been helping mighty good in the fields lately and he hunts at night. He needs to sleep."

"Maybe he could let up on hunting."

"Pa always said he got more work out of Nat if he let him have time out to hunt. Want me to call the kids to breakfast?"

"In a minute. Joel, you want to go up the river with Mr. Roubeau, don't you?"

"I had planned on it."

"And if you do—?"

"I know. You are wondering what will become of you and the little ones if I do. Well, I am wondering what will become of you if I don't."

"But Joel! We will be separated!"

"I know, Hannah," Joel said gently. "But keeping house and taking care of the little ones is a mighty big load for you to carry."

"Oh, but I can do it! I can do it!" Hannah cried. "Anything is better than breaking up. Anything!"

"There is a debt against this place, Hannah. The eighty that the buildings are on was a land grant. But two years ago when Pa decided to buy the hundred and sixty next to it from the fur trader, Etienne Roi, the only way he could raise the money was to give Gideon Baxter a mortgage on the whole two hundred and forty. Pa paid a big price for that hundred and sixty—three and a half dollars an acre —but he thought it was worth it. He said that good land right on the river would never be any cheaper."

"How much do we owe?"

"Right now five hundred and sixty dollars. Next fall with the interest we will owe him six hundred and seventy-two dollars. Baxter charged Pa twenty per cent interest. Because of the drought last year Pa couldn't do any more than pay the interest and extend the loan for another year. Mr. Cambright says we may be able to hold Baxter off until next spring. But the only way I know to raise enough money to pay him is to go up the river with Pierre Roubeau."

"But Joel, wouldn't someone else lend us the money?"

"There aren't many people out here on the frontier with money to lend. I've done a man's work for years but the law says I am under age and there isn't anyone, Hannah, who is going to lend a bunch of kids five hundred and sixty dollars. With the land we've cleared and the good buildings on the place, old Baxter thinks it would be a good deal for him to foreclose on us."

"Why did Pa pay so much for Mr. Roi's land, Joel, when he could go a few miles back from the river and get another land grant?"

"Land close to the river is always more valuable, Hannah. It produces better and it is easy to ship your produce when you are close to the river. Now that the steamboats are making regular trips between St. Louis and Independence it will be more valuable than ever. Besides, Roi's land was next to ours."

"How much will you make by going up the river?"

"Roubeau will give me twenty-five per cent of the prime hides I bring in and says I should make at least four hundred dollars."

"But Joel suppose— that is—what if—?"

"What if I don't get back? That is a chance we take every day of our lives, Hannah. I could ride a horse to Sibley—it could throw me and break my neck; a timber rattler fifty feet from the house could strike me; I could slip my axe—"

"Joel, could we stay here while you go?"

"You mean just you and Nat and the little ones?"

Hannah nodded.

"I wouldn't like it."

"I would like it a whole lot better than living with Cassie Overton and sending Nat to the Biddles. And heaven only knows who would take Jack and Marty."

"It might be better to separate for a few months than to separate for good."

"Oh, Joel," Hannah cried, "if we separate we might never get back together."

Hannah sank into a hickory chair by the table and dropped her head in her arms.

Joel came to stand over her. "It isn't an easy choice to make, Hannah. For all my hankering to go West I had decided I wouldn't. Then when I saw how bent on getting this place Gideon Baxter was, I knew I had to do something."

"What's the matter?" Nat had come down the ladder so quietly they hadn't heard him.

"It—it's that Joel thinks he must go up the river —and that we must go here and yonder."

Nat moved closer, patted her shoulder awkwardly. Hannah was pleased and surprised. She couldn't remember when Nat had ever made any show of affection toward her. Usually when she cried, he had yanked her braids and called her crybaby.

"This isn't to my liking either," said Joel. "But sometimes you have to make a choice. Good or bad you have to make a choice one way or the other. Pa didn't like the idea of putting a mortgage on our home but he thought it was right to do it."

"What about the corn crop if you go, Joel?" asked Nat.

"It will be laid by before the middle of July and I could ask the neighbors to gather it and haul it to Sibley in return for the use of our teams and cow while I am gone. Mr. Cambright said that he would store it in his warehouse and ship it to St. Louis. With enough rain, the land we have cleared should make a thousand bushels. After we take out for our own needs we should have seven hundred bushels to sell. Then if I bring back four hundred dollars to add to it we can pay Baxter off and tell him to go to grass."

"I guess there would be those who would take Nat and me in for our work and the Hopkins would keep little Angie, but what about Jack and Marty?"

"Well, after all, Hannah, we do have several kind-hearted neighbors. I would ask some of them to look after Jack and Marty."

"But I don't want someone to take them in like little waifs!" Hannah broke out in a fresh burst of tears. "And I don't want to work for anyone but my own family."

"Me neither," said Nat. "I'll go live with the Indians first."

Joel, a harassed look on his face, spoke hoarsely. "Listen, you kids. It's for a roof over your heads and the bread in your mouths that I am working. Don't make it any harder than it is already."

Nat shoved his hands deep in the pockets of his homespun jeans and looked at Joel squarely. "I don't see any reason why the rest of us can't stay right here while you go up the river."

"Nat, you don't mean it!" Hannah jumped out of her chair.

"Why not? I've been doing a man's work for the last two years—what time I wasn't hunting. The hay will be in and the corn laid by before Joel leaves. With a little help I can gather the corn and I know I can keep meat on the table next winter. I can start the plowing next spring and Joel will be home by planting time. I can hold up the outside end of it if Hannah can cook and look after the younger ones."

"The younger ones can help, too. Marty's eight and willing. Jack is nearly six. When I was eight I was helping Ma put out big washings."

Joel smiled ruefully. "I don't like the idea but I guess we can think about it."

Hannah ran into the other room. "Get up, Marty. We'll have breakfast and talk about how maybe we can stay together."

Marty rubbed her eyes, rolled out of bed. "Let's call Jack."

After Joel and Nat had gone to the field, Hannah talked seriously to Jack and Marty.

"Joel is going to have to go up the river with Mr. Roubeau to make money to pay Mr. Baxter. He doesn't want to leave us here. He is afraid we can't manage for ourselves. Now we've got to show him that we can work and pull together and you kids will have to help. You will have to mind, too."

Marty's eyes widened. "Why, Hannah, I always mind."

"Yes you do, Marty, and Jack must, too."

"I can mind if I have to," said Jack, his impish little face completely sober.

"Well, you'll have to, young man, if you don't want to go live with someone else," Hannah said firmly. "Besides, if you don't, I'll turn you across my apron."

"What do you want us to do, Hannah?" Marty asked.

"You can help me make the beds and sweep the floors and Jack can slop the pigs and bring up water from the spring—take two small pails instead of the big one. After that we will all go out to weed the onion bed. Then you and Jack can churn while I get dinner. Tomorrow we ought to hoe the green beans and plant black-eyed peas."

At noon when Joel and Nat came in from the field, the cabin was clean, the beds neatly fluffed and a good meal of rabbit stew, wild greens, new turnips and corn bread was on the table. Hannah and Jack and Marty were waiting with their faces and hands freshly washed and their hair neatly combed.

Halfway through the meal Joel said, "You are a good cook, Hannah."

Hannah smiled. "Jack and Marty helped. They pulled the turnips and peeled them and made the butter."

"That's good."

Nat made no comment but he didn't say anything to tease her. Always before when she had made the corn bread, Nat would tell her he found rocks in it; or if she had gathered the greens, he would tell Jack not to eat them, that there might be poison weeds in them. He ate quietly and when Joel got up to go back to the field Nat said nothing about wanting to hunt or fish, just followed Joel out the door and picked up his hoe.

Two weeks passed and although she missed Ma every hour of the day and she dreaded to see the boys come in without Pa, and the cabin seemed strangely quiet with only one little boy instead of two, the time moved surprisingly fast. Mr. Cambright had ridden by twice and Seth Newton had stopped on his way to the mill. Lizzie Brown and her two girls, Jane and Ephaniah, had spent an afternoon with them, and Bert Brown, who was Nat's age, had spent a day helping Nat clean the barn and the chicken house. Mrs. Cambright had sent a cured ham and a jug of molasses, and the Blackburns had come by on Sunday in their wagon to take them to the little Six Mile church.

Joel had made the five-mile trip back into the woods to see how little Angie was faring. On his return he reported that little Angie was well and happy and the Hopkins seemed pleased to have her.

Mr. Cambright came by early one morning and asked Joel to ride in to Independence with him. When they returned, Joel told Hannah that on the following Sunday afternoon some of the neighbors planned to come again. They would not come until after dinner, but Joel thought it would be nice if she had something to serve. Hannah thought so, too, because that was what Ma would have done. So on Saturday afternoon she baked a big batch of molasses cakes. She made them the way Ma had taught her, being careful to measure exactly. Jack and Marty brought corncobs for a quick fire so that the oven would get hot in a hurry and the cakes would rise rapidly. They came out of the brick oven light as a feather. Hannah was as proud as punch. She couldn't remember that Ma's were ever any nicer.

Grandma Peabody was the first to arrive the next

afternoon, and immediately after Gideon Baxter rode up.

"We could do without him," Nat growled.

"We certainly could," Hannah agreed. "But we must be polite. Remember he is a guest in our home."

"I just want to make sure it stays ours."

"The best way to do that, Nat," Hannah told him, "is to show him how much of a man you can be. Pa always said that a real man never shot off his mouth."

The women came into the cabin and the men sat down outside under the oak and maple trees. All the women complimented Hannah on her housekeeping, and the men told Joel and Nat that their corn and wheat looked thrifty. The Hopkins were a little late getting there and Hannah had begun to fear they might not come when they rode up. Little Angie wasn't so fresh as Ma had kept her but she was happy and her little face was round and pink.

Outside, the men talked crops and politics until Gideon Baxter cleared his throat and spoke above everyone else.

"Well, now you better bring the women out here because I reckon some of them will want a say in this."

Joel came to the door and asked the women to step outside.

Gideon cleared his throat again, "Well, now, as

I've been thinkin' there is just one way to handle this sad business, and that is to divide up these young'uns and do the best we can by 'em."

Hannah's face blanched, then turned slowly red. She pressed her lips firmly and watched.

"Were you intending to take any of them, Gideon?" Mr. Cambright asked.

"Well, now, I—that is—seeing as how I live some distance from here it might be better if folks closer by took 'em so that they could see each other more often."

"Then how about your taking all of them, Gideon?" Mr. Cambright persisted. "Separating children is a bad thing. You have a large house, your children are grown and married."

"Well—now—of course—that would be right nice, but my wife—well—she is kinda poorly right now."

"Is that so? She was in my store last week. She looked right spry to me."

"Well, now, Cambright, fact 'tis, my wife and me, we've raised one family and that ought to be enough for any couple."

"Indeed it is, Gideon. Anyone here will agree with you on that point. And that might be one reason for leaving these young people right where they are, especially since there is one of them past eighteen and willing to keep them here. Is that right, Joel?"

Hannah caught her breath and waited, her eyes

strained on Joel. He had never said—and so much hung on his decision.

Joel glanced first at Mr. Cambright, then straight at Gideon Baxter, his gray eyes steady, his jaw set. "That is right."

Gideon Baxter snorted. "Craziest thing I ever heard of! Leaving a bunch of kids to fend for themselves."

"I don't know what is so crazy about it," Seth Newton spoke up. "Lots of kids have been left worse off. They have a good farm here. Once they get it all cleared, it will be productive. They have a good cabin and stout buildings. They are all healthy and there are two young fellows here that have been hitting the heavy for several years. Give 'em a chance. Nothing crazy about that."

"The way things look around here none of them are afraid of work," said Mordecai Brown, then looking at his wife, "What do you women say?"

"They are young," Lizzie said hesitantly, "and a mother always hates to think of young ones being left alone without someone to watch over them—but breaking them up is bad, too."

"They seem to have done quite well, so far," said Mrs. Cambright. "I doubt that any of our houses are cleaner, and I just heard you men tell Joel and Nat how well their crops are doing."

Cassie Overton spoke, "I'm just like Mr. Baxter. It doesn't make sense to let children stay by themselves. Now I've already said I would take Hannah and Mr. Biddle here said he would take Nat."

"Shore did."

"Now that sounds like sense," said Gideon.

"Sounds to me like they are looking out for themselves instead of the kids," said George Blackburn.

"I think it is time that we ask these young people what they want to do," said Mr. Cambright. "After all it concerns them more than anyone else. Joel has already expressed his opinion. Now what do you think, Nat?"

Nat stood as solid as a block, his young face sober. "I say we can do it. I want to stay right here."

Hannah, standing by the doorway, was amazed at how square his jaw looked, how firm his voice was, and he was almost as broad-shouldered as Joel. What was it Ma had said? Someday Nat would grow up all of a sudden and maybe this was the moment.

"A fourteen-year-old boy is too young to have an opinion," Gideon grumbled.

But Mr. Cambright ignored him. "Hannah, what have you to say?"

Hannah blushed at having all the eyes focused on her, but she didn't hesitate.

"I don't see any reason why we can't stay here. We can manage and I think that is what Ma and Pa would want us to do."

"What about you, little lady? What do you want to do?" he asked Mary.

Marty gripped a fold of Hannah's skirt and, with her head bent in timidity, said, "I want to be wherever Hannah is and I'd rather stay at home."

"And you, young fellow?" he said, drawing Jack up on his knee.

Jack looked around at his red-headed hero and said, "I want to stay with Nat."

"I think that makes it unanimous," said Mr. Cambright.

Gideon Baxter's face turned red. "Unanimous indeed! A bunch of kids who don't know what they want. I might just as well speak my piece. As some of you undoubtedly know, I hold a mortgage on this place and—"

"So that's it." Bill Moore, who had said nothing up to now, spoke, and his voice was belittling. "You had interests beyond the welfare of the orphans."

"You might call it that."

"We all know it, Gideon," George Blackburn said. "You weren't kidding any of us."

"Well, I can't afford to let a bunch of kids run this place down."

"These young people can't afford to let it run down either, and I think they know it," said Mr. Cambright.

"That's your opinion, Alf. I say they will and I can't afford to let that happen. I'll have to foreclose."

Seth Newton jumped to his feet, his face blazing.

"That would be a good deal for you, Gideon Baxter, with these good buildings on the place, a nice piece of land cleared and a good meadow, besides. You are one of the few men in the country who would do it."

"He is lousy enough to, all right," Dave Powell grumbled.

"I don't lend money for pastime."

"Nobody borrows from you for pastime!" Mordecai Brown shot back.

"Gentlemen! Gentlemen!" Mr. Cambright stood up and Hannah thought how dignified he looked in his black broadcloth suit and his white poplin vest. "No need to get riled. Mr. Baxter cannot foreclose immediately. It will be at least a year."

"I can call in my money when it falls due in October."

"Since you are going to have to live within the law for the most part, Gideon, it would pay you to study it a little more. This territory hasn't been a state many years, but the men who wrote the laws took precaution to protect orphans and property."

"I reckon I've got a right to call in my money."

"Not in an estate. The law says that a debt cannot be collected for twelve months from the time the estate is filed for probate and where there are minors it takes a little longer."

"And just why does it take longer?" demanded Gideon.

"There are a few decisions to make, such as appointing a guardian and having him approved by the court, then the guardian files the estate in behalf of the minors."

"Since I am more interested in this property than anyone else, perhaps I can be appointed guardian."

"You are too late, Gideon," said Mr. Cambright. "Joel and I have already gone before the court in Independence and asked that I be appointed guardian for these children."

"And what interest have you, sir?"

"To see that these young people get a square deal."

Gideon rose hastily, went over to the tree where his horse was tied and climbed into the saddle.

"You may have bitten off more than you can chew, Cambright."

"I may have but I'll take my chances."

As soon as Gideon had ridden off, Seth Newton turned to Joel.

"Joel, since you want to hold the family together, do you think you should go up the river?"

Joel looked at the big oak on the other side of the yard before he spoke. "I've thought so much about it I can't sleep nights and the only answer I find is to go up the river. Owing to the drought last year, we raised very little more than enough corn to feed ourselves and the stock. Pa wasn't able to pay off more than the interest. I had hoped at first that Mr. Baxter might be induced to take the interest and a part payment and extend the loan."

"Not Baxter," said Mordecai Brown. "He wants this place."

"What kind of proposition did Roubeau offer you?"

"Twenty-five per cent of my take and he says that I ought to make at least four hundred dollars. With that much I think we can finish paying off the mortgage with corn. We have had good rains so far this year and if we get a little more in the tasseling season, we ought to harvest a thousand bushels."

"Some of those traders are pretty crooked," said George Blackburn. "That is half the cause of the Indian trouble."

"Roubeau is honest. He seldom has any trouble with the Indians, just a brush now and then."

At this point Hannah went into the cabin and brought out two platters of molasses cakes, then sent Jack and Marty to the springhouse for pitchers of cool milk. The baby, who had slept in her cradle, woke and started kicking and cooing. Hannah took her out of the cradle and kissed her. She and Marty took turns holding her, but when she got hungry she held out her arms to Maggie.

"Hannah, my dear," said Lizzie Brown as she was leaving, "I think it might be well to let Maggie take the baby back with her. It might help to fill the summer for Maggie and you are going to have all you can do."

Hannah looked at Maggie and the baby. If Maggie was just a little more particular. And Skip—well, he was just a man who had dragged his family from pillar to post. They had lived in a squatter's hut on the river for a time, they had lived in a shanty in Sibley and now they were living five miles back in the timber. Yet Maggie was kind and she and Skip were both attached to the baby and Angie was thriving.

"I think perhaps you should, too," Essie Newton said. "It isn't easy to bring a baby through the hot weather, especially if you are trying to raise it on a bottle."

Hannah looked at Grandma Peabody.

"They are probably right, Hannah. They have both had several babies to bring through the summer."

"Why don't you leave her until there has been a good killing frost?" Anna Moore suggested.

"We would sure like to have her," said Maggie, looking down at the baby and running her fingers through the soft reddish gold ringlets.

"We'll take jest as good care of her as if she wuz our own," said Skip. "In fact, we would like to keep her for good."

"Oh, no! No!" Hannah cried and made a move to take the baby from Maggie.

Joel spoke up quickly. "We aren't giving our little sister to anyone, Skip, but if you and Maggie want to keep her through the summer, it looks to me as if it might be a good thing."

"We want to keep her all right," said Maggie.

So Hannah, with a lump in her throat, watched Skip and Maggie ride off through the woods with little Angie.

CHAPTER V

THE DAYS that followed were busy ones, with Nat and Joel in the field at sunrise, working from daylight till dark to lay by the corn and get in the hay before Joel went up the river. Joel had made arrangements with Scott Allison at Blue Mills to cradle the wheat when it was ready. Hannah's days were full, too. She was up before daylight to fix a good breakfast for Joel and Nat. Then she would call Jack and Marty and as soon as they had eaten, she would send Jack to slop the pigs and carry water. Nat had carved a small yoke and attached two small cedar buckets to it. It made Jack feel big to go off to the spring with a yoke across his shoulders. While Jack did these chores, Hannah and Marty made the beds, swept the floors and tidied the kitchen. After the housework was done, usually they worked in the garden. The beans, the okra and squash were bearing. The green peas had been used, the vines pulled and parsnips for winter use planted in their place. Joel and Nat had planted a large patch of beans for drying and shelling at the edge of the cornfield. Next month they would pull the winter onions and tie them and hang them from rafters in the loft.

Hannah was proud of not having to ask Joel and Nat to help with anything in the house and garden. She and Jack and Marty had taken care of everything except digging the potatoes. Joel wouldn't let them do that. That was too big a job for girls, he said. He and Nat dug them and she and Jack and Marty had picked them up and put them in gunny sacks. When they had finished and Nat and Joel had carried them to the root cellar, Joel had estimated that they had put away fourteen bushels for winter.

One afternoon before he left, Joel said they would all go to Sibley. Hannah was pleased, as she always enjoyed a trip to Sibley. They would go to Mr. Cambright's store and buy supplies. Joel wanted them to have the things they needed for winter before he left. Joel hitched the team, January and June, to the wagon, but Nat wanted to ride Belle, Pa's riding horse. Jack and Marty were so delighted they jumped up and down in the wagonbed as they bumped along on the deeply rutted wagon trail. They stopped for a while at Grandma Peabody's where Nat was waiting for them, then went on to Cambright's store.

Joel tied the team at the hitching rack and they all climbed out and went around to the steps that led up to the roofed porch that ran the full length of the building. Mr. Cambright was talking to his clerk, Ephraim Locke, but he left off and came over to speak to them.

"So the whole family came this time."

"Yes," said Joel. "I wanted Hannah to get the supplies she will need and I wanted you to take an order for boots for all of them for next winter. When the corn is gathered, Nat will bring in enough to pay you."

Mr. Cambright nodded. "That will be fine."

Hannah always loved coming to Cambright's store. She liked the clean smell of the whitewashed walls, mingled with the aroma that came from the barrels of coffee beans and molasses. She enjoyed looking around at the neatly stacked bolts of muslin, calico and twilled cotton. At one side was the case for thread and another larger case which held ribbons and lace. Back of them were slates, spellers and a few readers. Brass kettles, pots and pans lined the walls opposite the barrels of beans and sugar. Joel went to the back of the store where tools and plows were kept, and Nat stood gazing admiringly at Mr. Cambright's fine Kentucky rifle that hung over the door. Jack and Marty looked longingly at the end of the counter that was covered with curved glass where the peppermint sticks, horehound drops and other sweetmeats were kept. The big wheel of yellow cheese in its glass cage looked rich and tempting.

Ephraim Locke measured their feet, then had each one of them stand on a piece of brown paper while he drew around their feet with a quill pen. Mr. Cambright said that the next time he went to Independence he would take the measurements and the outlines to the cobbler to make lasts and to cobble shoes for them before cold weather.

Hannah, with Lizzie Brown's help, had made out her list. She would have loved a length of the sprigged calico for dresses for herself and Marty but Lizzie had counseled her to hold her lists to absolute necessities. They could make do with their last year's calicoes for the rest of the summer, and for the winter Lizzie and Grandma Peabody had offered to help loom homespun cloth for dresses and jeans and shirts as Ma had always done. So Hannah ordered a bolt of flannel to make winter clothes for little Angie and petticoats for herself and Marty, flannel underwear for all of them; salt, soda, baking powder, coffee beans, a small amount of rice and, after some hesitancy, she added ten pounds of loaf sugar and a little arrowroot for puddings.

Mr. Cambright complimented Hannah on her selections and as they were leaving, he handed her a small bag which he said they were to open on the way home. They were no more than settled in the wagonbed and started than Jack and Marty made her open the bag. It was filled with peppermint sticks and horehound drops. The children jumped up and down, squealing with joy, and Jack rammed his chubby fist to the bottom of the sack but Hannah said they must be divided. She gave Jack and Marty the biggest portions and insisted that Joel take a share, then she called to Nat to ride up close so that she could hand some to him.

It was a pleasant ride home and it gave Hannah a good feeling to know that they had their supplies from the store laid in.

On the fourteenth of July, Pierre Roubeau's flatboats tied up below old Fort Osage around the bend from the warehouses at the Sibley wharves. He immediately sent word to Joel and Joel went down to Sibley to talk with him. Mr. Roubeau had been shocked and saddened, Joel said on his return, at the news of the death of their parents and Sammie. Mr. Roubeau would go on to Wayne City landing to take on supplies from Independence and Joel was to be in camp the following night in order to start at dawn the next day.

Hannah got Joel's pack in order. He had already cleaned and oiled Pa's rifle and had it ready along with the pouch and powder horn. The old breech-loading flintlock was to be left for Nat. Hannah knew that Nat preferred the rifle but Nat understood that it was necessary for Joel to have the best gun and he had not complained.

Hannah had made a pack of two homespun blankets, a linsey shirt and red flannel underwear, and a pair of extra-heavy wool knitted socks that Grandma Peabody had sent. Since it would be the last supper that Joel would have at home before he left, Hannah wanted to fix extra. Joel and Nat had taken off work before noon so that Joel could get down to see Mr. Roubeau and Nat had gone fishing. After Joel had come back to tell them he would be leaving the next day he had ridden off to talk to a few neighbors— Seth Newton, Mordecai Brown and George Blackburn. Mr. Cambright and Grandma Peabody he had seen in Sibley that morning. After that, he rode over to the Hopkins to make sure all was well with little Angie.

Nat not only brought in pan-sized catfish for supper but dressed them without being asked. That gave Hannah more time for the rest of the meal. Nat did the chores by himself so that there would be nothing for Joel to do when he came in. It gave Hannah a good feeling that Nat was growing more thoughtful. She wasn't going to mind being left with him half as much as she had thought.

Hannah sent Jack and Marty to the garden for green beans and new cabbage which she cooked with the last of the hog's jowl left from last winter's butchering. She scrubbed potatoes and put them in the ashes to roast, fried the fish, made a pan of corn bread and brought out a small crock of honey from a bee tree that Nat had found.

Joel had come in late, looking tired, but said that he had found little Angie well and happy. They were just ready to sit down when someone rode up and called out.

Joel went to the door. "Pierre Roubeau! What brings you to the woods?"

"My good friend's family."

"Come in. We are just ready to eat."

"Then I am fortunate—if it be no inconvenience to young mademoiselle—what is her name?"

"Hannah," said Joel. "And this is the younger girl, Marty."

"How do you do," said Hannah and Marty together.

"Oh yes, I remember. And here is young Nat, the hunter. I do believe you have added a little height and breadth, Nat, just since April."

He carried a new Kentucky rifle which he stood in the corner by the fireplace. Nat looked at it admiringly. As far back as he could remember he had wanted a Kentucky rifle.

"And here is my friend, little Jack." . . . Only he pronounced it "Jacques."

Jack made a leap toward him and Pierre swung him in the air.

Hannah, remembering her place as hostess, said what Ma always said to unexpected company, "If you will take pot luck with us, Mr. Roubeau, it will pleasure us no little."

"Thank you, mademoiselle, the pleasure is all mine and I shall be happy to share such a fine supper as you have here, but first, may I wash the dirt of the trail from my hands and face?"

Joel poured water into the washbasin on the stand by the door and gave him a piece of Ma's homemade soap and Hannah brought a homespun flax-linen towel.

"But, yes," said Pierre. "The news you gave me stayed with me all afternoon so that when we had gone upstream as far as Blue Mills I tied up to talk a bit with your father's friend, Monsieur Rice, keeper of the mill. Then it came to my mind that your father's farm lay about halfway between Sibley and Blue Mills. So I left my crew at Blue Mills landing, borrowed a horse from Monsieur Rice, rode back and here I am with the added pleasure of a fine meal before me."

As he ate, Pierre Roubeau talked. "A wise man your father was and one to see well ahead. Like all

Welshmen he loved the land. It is a good thing to buy a farm between two good river landings—a prosperous town like Sibley and a booming place like Blue Mills—and Independence only fourteen miles upstream. With more and more people coming West and the steamboats making regular trips between St. Louis and Independence, these Missouri settlements will grow."

"If there were only a little more money to help us buy land and get started," said Joel.

"Yes," said Pierre. "The Santa Fe trade brings dollars into Independence but as yet it has brought no dollars to the farmers—still it may."

"Not soon enough to do us any good."

"Not just yet, but when more people move into Independence and there is a need for it, they will build a farmer's market like the one in St. Louis. Then the farmer can take that which he does not need for his own table to the market in Independence, and Independence housewives will come to buy and pay in silver for the farmer's lard and butter and eggs and poultry."

"How funny," said Hannah, "to think of buying or selling such things as butter or eggs. That is something that almost anyone has or can borrow from a neighbor."

Pierre smiled. "Yes, Mademoiselle Hannah, in this land of plenty in the good Missouri Valley all those

who are willing to work can eat well, set a table"—
he made a gesture with his hand—"such as this.
Where the woods are full of fish and game as well
as fruits and nuts, a man can live well. If he is fortunate enough to have an industrious wife to raise the
garden and poultry and keep a clean house, he can
live like a king. But he still needs money to buy
land."

Pierre pushed back his chair, filled his pipe and
took Jack on his knee. Hannah and Marty cleared
the dishes off the table and as soon as they had finished, Pierre took out his jew's harp. He played
several lively tunes that were unfamiliar to them,
then in a deep, pleasant voice he sang for them. They
were all French songs and they couldn't understand
the words but they loved the rhythm of them and
before they knew it he had them all singing along
with him.

> *A-lou-et-te*
> *Gen-tille a-lou-et-te*
> *A-lou-et-te*
> *Je te plu-me-rai*

Then they ended up with:

> *Viva le viva le viva le morte*
> *Viva le viva le viva le morte*
> *Viva le morte viva le morte*
> *Viva le compagne.*

After a time he got to his feet. "Well, *mes enfants*, the moon is up, a perfect lantern in the sky to light me on the trail. Thank you, mademoiselle, for the very good meal," he said, bowing to Hannah.

Hannah blushed and smiled. "Oh, but you were so welcome, sir."

"Can't you stay the night, sir?" said Joel.

"Thank you, no. We must go on to the Wayne City landing very early tomorrow so that I can go in to Independence and buy my supplies for the trip up the river and get loaded before dark."

He placed a hand on Marty's dark curls. "You are fortunate to have a sister who is so much a woman at her young age. And, Nat, it is good to know that you are willing to take on a man's responsibility. I have brought you a present to help you—shall we say—keep the wolf from the door?"

He went to the corner and picked up the long Kentucky rifle and handed it to Nat. Nat stood spellbound, unable to believe his ears. Slowly, incredulously, he reached out and took the rifle from Pierre, ran his hand caressingly over the curly maple wood of the stock. It had open sights, both front and rear, fixed to the barrel by a grooved slide, and, like all Kentucky rifles, there was an eight-point brass star sunk into the chunk piece on the left side.

"You don't mean you are giving it to me?"

"Yes, it will make up in part for my taking your

elder brother from you. Keep it clean, oil it often, and it will serve you for many years."

"But the gift is too much," Joel protested.

Pierre made a deprecating gesture. "Your father in his time befriended me more largely than that. As your frontier people put it so nicely, it will pleasure me to give it to Nat."

"For sure, it will pleasure me to use it," said Nat. "A Kentucky rifle!" His voice was full of awe.

"Then that is full pay, young man."

"Thank you, sir," said Joel. "It is most generous."

"Yes, thank you, thank you indeed," said Nat.

"Well, I must be on my way. I shall see you in camp tomorrow night, Joel."

They followed him outside, Nat clutching the rifle. Pierre Roubeau rode off up the trail in the light of the moon. At the far edge of the meadow, where the trail led through the woods, he looked back and raised his hand. Nat lifted his precious gun in salute.

"Good-bye. Come again," they all called after him.

CHAPTER VI

JOEL DIDN'T LEAVE until mid-afternoon of the next day. Nat thought he should ride.

"No need to walk, Joel. I could ride over with you. One of us could ride January and the other could ride June or Belle, and I could lead your horse back."

"No, I'm a fast walker. If you go, it would make you out after dark and I don't want you away from the girls at night. Remember, you are the man of the place."

Nat squared his shoulders. "Don't worry, Joel. I'll remember."

"No need to tell you to take good care of the little ones Hannah. I know you will." He patted Marty's head and pulled Jack's ear. "Be a good boy, Jack, and do everything Hannah tells you to."

They all walked with him to the edge of the meadow and stood watching as he walked swiftly up the trail.

'Good-bye. Good luck."

He entered the woods and the trees closed behind him

As they turned back to the cabin, there was a heaviness in their hearts that none of them spoke of It was past the middle of the afternoon and Nat didn't want to go back to the field alone.

'I think I will go out and get us some fresh meat," he said.

Hannah knew he was itching to try out his new rifle. "I think that would be a good idea. Try to get some prairie chickens."

Nat whistled for Zip and set off toward the woods. "I'll be back by dark."

There was nothing in the house or garden that needed immediate attention and there were at least four more hours of daylight. Hannah thought this might be a good time to dig buck-brush roots. Last spring when she had spent a few days with Grandma Peabody, Grandma had taught her which roots to gather for basket weaving, how to boil them and peel off the rough outer bark and weave them into baskets. Their reed baskets were almost worn out and Hannah had been wanting to weave a few out of buck brush. Nat would not be home for several hours; so, to make a little occasion that would take the children's minds off Joel's leaving, she packed a picnic. There was a spring under a bluff where buck brush grew; they could eat their supper there. She would like to go by the graves and leave some wild roses, but she knew Jack and Marty would cry if she did. She would slip over some morning before they were out of bed and take flowers.

They found buck brush in abundance on the bluff and Hannah selected a spot where she thought it would be easier to dig. First she loosened the dirt around a clump, then she chopped the bushes down to the ground and had Jack and Marty carry them out of the way. The digging turned out to be harder than she had expected. It was slow, hard work and she had to rest between spells. Jack and Marty helped as best they could by chopping the earth with the hatchet.

After more than two hours of digging and chopping, Hannah thought they had enough. They gathered up the roots, put them in the hamper and took down the bag of food that Hannah had tied to a hickory branch for safekeeping and went down under the bluff to eat. They spread their supper on a big flat rock and seated themselves beside the spring. It was cool and comfortable there with a soft breeze playing in the tops of the trees. The tinkling of the water running down the bluff and over the rocks made a pleasant sound. As they ate, Hannah noticed with satisfaction that Marty was picking up a little in weight.

It was when they were about half through their meal that Hannah had a peculiar feeling of being watched. She looked up, glanced around, but saw nothing. She continued eating, but the peaceful pleasure she had felt a moment ago was gone. She found herself looking around now and then. Once she even turned and looked behind her.

"What's the matter, Hannah?"

"Oh, nothing, Marty. Just—well—I don't know."

Jack and Marty wanted to swing on the wild grapevines, but Hannah said they should be getting home. She wanted Jack and Marty to carry up water from the spring below the cabin and fill the washkettle in the back yard so that she could start boiling the buckbrush roots first thing in the morning. Besides, she thought she should do the milking since Nat would probably not be in much before dark.

They walked the short distance from the woods to the cabin in a few minutes. Jack and Marty fed the chickens and went off to the spring under the hill for water and Hannah took the milkpail and went to the barn. As usual, Betsey was at the far end of the pasture, but at least she was in sight. Pa had never been one to turn his stock loose in the woods. He and Joel had split rails and fenced in the pasture the first year they lived here.

"Saw, Betsey—saw, Betsey—saw—saw," Hannah called.

Betsey took her time but the horses came running. The sheep and the oxen on the other side of the pasture raised their heads, looked at her and went back to cropping grass. The wagon team, January and June, and Belle, Pa's riding horse, came trotting up to her. She went back to the crib and got a nubbin of corn for each of them. She held open the gate and Betsey meandered in, brushing flies with her tail.

Jack and Marty had just come in with their second load of water when she came in from milking.

"I'm tired, Hannah," said Jack. "Can't we wait 'til morning to fill the kettle?" His lips trembled. "I wish Ma was here," he whimpered. The tears gathered in Marty's large brown eyes and rolled down her cheeks.

"Of course we can," said Hannah. "Come wash your feet and put on your night shirt, and as soon as I take the milk to the springhouse, I will tell you a story."

Hannah came back from the springhouse hurriedly, wishing for the first time in her life that Nat was around the house. She sat down in the rocker, took Jack on her lap and pulled up the footstool for Marty.

"Tell us about Bluebeard."

"Oh, no," Marty protested. "Tell us about the prince and the sleeping beauty."

"Well, once upon a time—" Hannah started off, then stopped.

"Go on, Hannah. What's the matter?"

Hannah leaned forward, started to get up, spilling Jack from her lap, then immediately jerked back again and at the same time put a hand out to Marty. How could it be? There was no sound to warn her; the dog, of course, was off with Nat. Just all at once the doorway darkened and three big Indians came in. There they stood, dark and oily and unbelievably dirty, looking around with solemn, curious eyes. Like the Little Osage, they wore only breechcloths and their heads were shaved except for a bristling ridge down the center, but around their necks were strings of beads which the local Indians never wore. One appeared to be older. He wore heavy rings in his slitted ears and a wampum belt around his middle. Ma said that when Indians came into your cabin they were hungry; given food, they would leave.

"Who are they?" said Jack, but Marty did not open her mouth and Hannah knew she was frightened. Without a word, Hannah got up, went to the safe and spread big hunks of corn bread with butter and handed it to them. They walked around the cabin eating, poking into everything. It was all Hannah could do to keep from shouting at them to get out. They opened the chest drawers and pulled out clothing—Marty's little petticoats and Jack's waists. These they threw on the floor. But when one of them came upon Pa's red flannel underwear laid away in the bottom drawer he grinned broadly and tied it around his waist. Meanwhile, the other young one was plucking turkey feathers out of Ma's duster. The older one seemed less curious, or perhaps he was looking for something more valuable.

Jack and Marty stood behind Hannah, clinging to her skirts. Hannah drew in her breath and tried to decide whether she should gather the children and run or stand and act as if she wasn't afraid. All of a sudden she thought of Pa's old flintlock over the door. Could she get past the older one and snatch it?

While she was trying to decide, the older Indian made a move toward the door. Perhaps he had seen her look toward the gun and was going to outmaneuver her. At any rate, he reached up and took down Pa's old flintlock. He ran his hand over the stock, examined it curiously while Hannah held her breath and Jack and Marty gripped her skirts. Would he aim it at them? Would he shoot them? Hannah stood frozen, her heart pounding like a hammer. She gritted her teeth to keep them from chattering, tightened her grip on the trembling children. He lifted the gun and sighted through it. Hannah's face blanched, her fingers turned to ice. Oh! If Mr. Brown or Nat, even Amos Biddle—anyone—would walk in! With a great gulp of relief, she saw him put the gun over his shoulder and start to leave. On the step he looked back at the younger men, grunted, motioned to them to follow. He turned back, barked an order and went toward the barn. The other two followed.

Hannah, with Jack on one side and Marty on the other, watched from the door as the Indians passed the barn, opened the gate and started across the pasture.

"What are they going to do, Hannah?"

"I don't know." But she feared she did know.

As she expected, they made a beeline for the horses. The older one went after Belle and the younger ones caught January and June. They were through the gate and headed for the woods like a streak of lightning.

"Hannah! They are taking our horses!" Jack wailed. "What are we going to do?"

"That's just what I am wondering."

She thought of several things they might do. They might cut out through the woods to the Browns' who lived about a mile to the east toward Sibley. They could go up the wagon track from their farm to the Santa Fe Trail hoping that some rider they knew might come along, or they could just stay where they were and wait for Nat. In the end that was what they did, and though the time seemed endless, actually it was less than half an hour. They all ran to meet him as soon as they saw him coming out of the woods north of the clearing. Jack dashed ahead as fast as his sturdy little legs would carry him.

"Nat! Nat! Injuns stole our horses! And took Pa's gun and his red flannels."

"What are you talking about?"

"That's right. They—" All at once Hannah broke off in a sob. The day had been too much. "Oh, Nat, they took our horses." Her young body, seeking a shoulder to lean on, swayed toward Nat and found it.

Nat put his arm around her awkwardly. She was his sister, younger than he and looking to him for comfort. He had been called upon to act like a man. His arm around her tightened and all at once it wasn't awkward. In all his life he had never felt so close to her.

"What did they look like?"

It was Marty who answered. "Big and tall. They had bristle ridges."

"Osage?"

Hannah dried her eyes on her apron. "They looked

like them and had that bristle down the center of their heads like the Osage, but they wore more ornaments than the Osage around here."

"Which way did they go?"

"Through the south woods and west of the trail."

"I'll go right after them, the big bums." Then looking at the children and lowering his voice he said, "No, not yet. Let's go to the cabin. Jack and Marty, put your clothes back on." Then to Hannah, "You think they were Osage?"

"They looked like them."

"That's strange. I just never heard of an Osage around here taking more than a ham out of a smoke-house or a chicken off a roost, and only when they were mighty hungry at that." When they reached the cabin, he said, 'We'll go to the Browns'. You and the little ones can stay there and Mr. Brown and Bert and I will round up the neighbors to see if we can catch them. Hurry up, kids. We've got to move fast."

It was dark in the woods and frightening with the moon not yet up and brush closing behind them as they plunged through the bushes. Nat walked in front, feeling his way steadily. Hannah followed, holding tight to Marty's hand and pushing Jack ahead close between her and Nat. After what seemed like an endless time, the trees thinned out and they were in Browns' clearing.

"Hello, Mr. Brown," Nat called out. "Hello!"

"Hello, who's there?"

"Nat Harelson."

Mordecai and Bert came out of the cabin. Lizzie lighted a candle and came to the door, Jane and Ephaniah and the younger boys, Tom and Chris, behind her.

"What's the matter?"

"Three Indians stole our horses while I was out hunting."

"Stole your horses?"

"Stole your horses!" They all echoed behind him.

"Well, by all that is holy! That is strange. Indians around here don't give trouble. Come in."

"Yes, come in, my dears," said Lizzie. "Ephaniah, you and Jane go to the springhouse and fetch a pitcher of milk and bring some bread and butter."

"I don't care for anything to eat, Mrs. Brown," said Hannah, "but maybe Nat would. I was so worked up I plumb forgot he hadn't had any supper."

Nat shook his head. "I've got no time to eat. I thought maybe Mr. Brown would help me round up some neighbors to follow the Indians. Do you think we ought to send word to Joel?"

"Joel couldn't do anything more than any other man could do," said Mordecai. "He is going away with enough on his mind. I am not for adding anything to it. Your neighbors will help you, Nat. How long has it been?"

"Well, let's see," said Hannah. "It must have been half an hour before dark. I reckon it's been an hour and a half."

"Which way did they go?"

"Through the woods south of our cabin and west of the trail."

"And you didn't see anything of them, Nat?"

Nat shook his head. "I had been hunting northeast of the place."

"What did they look like?"

"They looked like the Osage, except that they wore a lot of beads and trinkets."

"That's the Arkansas Osage. A few of them drift up this way—just passing through—the ones that give trouble. They will be hard to catch up with. Well, let's saddle the horses, Bert. We'll go by Seth Newton's and on to Cambright's, but there is no telling where those confounded redskins are now. They've got a good start on us."

As soon as Nat and Mordecai and Bert rode off, Lizzie started tucking the rest of them in. She gave Hannah an extra pat. "Now don't worry, honey. In the end things usually work out."

Hannah gave a long, shuddering sigh, turned over and went to sleep.

The next morning Jane and ten-year-old Tom went home with Hannah to feed and milk, but Lizzie instructed them to hurry back.

"While we are here," said Jane, after they had carried the milk to the springhouse, "we will straighten up your cabin. Looks like those Indians played havoc."

Late in the afternoon the men came back, disheartened.

"We didn't see hide nor hair of them," said Bert, "and there were nine of us."

"Yes," said Mordecai, "we divided up and went in three directions, but not a trace of them did we find."

As soon as they had eaten, Bert resaddled the horses and took the Harelsons home. After the chores were done, it seemed strange for only the four of them to be there. Jack curled up on Ma's bed and went to sleep. Marty undressed and got into bed, and Nat climbed the ladder to the loft. Hannah lingered in the kitchen, brushed off the mantel, and swept the hearth, even though no cooking had been done. She was tempted to leave a candle burning but that was dangerous. Ma never did. Reluctantly, she blew out the candle, went into the bedroom, and undressed in the dark. Before she lay down beside Marty, she went back into the kitchen and stood in the doorway, looked out and stood listening for a moment. Slowly she closed the door and latched it. She lay down beside Marty but she couldn't sleeep. She raised herself on her elbow and looked around. When a mouse ran across the floor she jumped straight up. What was that noise? It must be Nat fumbling around in the loft. What could he be doing? Soon she heard him coming down the ladder dragging something after him.

"Nat," she called, "what are you doing?"

"I'm bringing this old buffalo robe down. I'm going to sleep here by the kitchen doorway, Hannah. I'll have my rifle beside me and Zip is out here by the doorstep. You go to sleep. There isn't anything going to hurt you and Jack and Marty."

Hannah knew that with Nat and his rifle between them and the door that nothing would hurt them. She lay back down by Marty and dropped off to sleep.

CHAPTER VII

THE NEXT DAY Nat took Jack to the bean patch with him to hoe. "He might as well learn," said Nat. "Joel and I started hoeing when we were his age."

Nat fitted a short handle into a light hoe and Jack walked off beside Nat with his hoe over his shoulder and feeling as big as Nat.

Early last fall Ma had them carry cornshucks to the barn loft to dry. If Nat was going to sleep on the floor, Hannah was going to give him something better than a buffalo robe for a summer bed.

"There is a piece of ticking in the bottom drawer of the chest that Ma bought last winter," Hannah said to Marty. "I think we can make a mattress for Nat out of cornshucks."

"If we make one, we had better make two," said Marty. "When Jack finds out Nat is sleeping on the floor, he is going to want to sleep on the floor, too. He is getting to be more like Nat's shadow every day."

Hannah laughed. Marty was a quiet little piece but when she spoke she hit the nail on the head. Marty was getting to be a lot of help. She was small for her age and slender but there was a wiriness about her that set a good pace. She was quick to catch on, too.

They started cutting and sewing. By splicing it with a heavy piece of unbleached muslin there was enough ticking to make a fair-sized mattress for Nat and a smaller one for Jack. They worked at it steadily, sewing with the neat little stitches Ma had taught them to use. With time out only for preparing dinner, they had both mattresses finished and stuffed with clean-smelling cornshucks before sundown.

Marty finished Jack's mattress by herself so that Hannah could do the milking. Nat would work late in the bean patch in order to finish. As Hannah came around the corner of the barn, a bucket of milk in her hand, she nearly dropped it at the sight of an Indian standing beside the cabin door. Nat and Jack were coming up the path from the bean patch. She stifled the scream that rose to her lips—it was only Sagameeshee.

Sagameeshee followed Nat into the cabin and sniffed at the leftover food which was warming in the pot over the coals.

Hannah set the pail of milk on the table, spoke politely to Sagameeshee. "Good evening, Sagameeshee. Will you have supper with us?"

Hannah knew that he didn't want to eat at the table with them. Pa said that he wasn't used to eating with women. Indian men always ate first, gathering around the fire and dipping their fingers into the pot. When they had finished, the women got the scraps. So Hannah heaped a plate with stewed squirrel and vegetables and corn bread and handed it to Sagameeshee and fixed another for Nat who followed him outside and sat with him on the ground.

As she and Jack and Marty ate, Hannah could hear Sagameeshee talk now and then in grunts and short sentences. After he had gone, Nat came back into the cabin.

"Mr. Brown was right. Sagameeshee said those Indians that stole our horses were Osage from the Arkansas band and there is no hope of getting them back. It was some of Big Track's bucks, he thinks. Big Track tries to keep the treaty with the government, but when any of his band come up here he can't do anything about them."

"I've heard Pa speak of Big Track," said Hannah. "He said he was respected by both whites and Indians.

Didn't Pa say that he came up here one time to work out a treaty with the government?"

"Yes, but those Indians that rove sell the horses before they return to the tribe and there is nothing Big Track can do about it."

The summer days, filled with a busy routine, passed more rapidly than Hannah had thought they could. They planted peas and green beans for the fall garden. Later they planted turnips and parsnips for storing, referring, of course, to Ma's almanac to be sure that they planted them when the sign was right.

Grandma Peabody came to spend a week and help finish the sewing Ma and Hannah had started before Ma got sick. Hannah wondered how it was that Grandma Peabody could fill a house with so much cheer. She didn't laugh a lot, or talk loud. She just buzzed, finding a dozen things to do about the place and giving orders to everybody. Soon everyone was busy and happy.

She would snap at Nat if he dared sit down at the table without combing his unruly locks. "Nat, you big clodhopper, you've been taught better than that! Get up and comb your hair."

And Nat, grinning, would get up and comb his hair.

Then when they were all seated and she had asked a blessing, she would start right off with a round of entertaining stories. She always knew all the community news because everyone stopped at her house coming and going. Grandma had a raft of stories, too—stories of her youth, of bee hunts, Indian raids, quilting parties and dances.

Grandma had come to the Boone's Lick country as a young woman with her husband. Later they had come on up to Fort Osage after Captain Sibley had established the trading post for Indians. Grandma never tired of talking about Captain Sibley's beautiful and talented wife, Mary, who had come up the river as a bride of fifteen and brought the first piano west of the Mississippi.

"Did the Sibleys have much company out here in the wilderness?"

"Oh, my, yes. The Sibleys were the most hospitable people in the world. There were lots of notables among the voyagers up the Missouri in those days—Mr Catlin, that artist that painted pictures of the Indians, and Mr. Audubon that painted pictures of birds. There was even a prince—Prince Maximilian."

"A prince!" Hannah gasped. "What did he look like?"

"Oh, about like all the other voyagers—doeskin leggings and a dirty hunting shirt and a month's growth of whiskers on his face. Only he looked a little worse than most, maybe because he had no teeth."

' A prince without teeth wouldn't be very romantic, but just imagine any kind of prince being in Sibley," said Hannah.

"There was no such town as Sibley then—just the

fort. There was a treaty with the Indians to guarantee the safety of any settlers within six square miles of the fort. That's why this neighborhood is called the Six Mile Territory. Well—" Grandma broke off, "let's clear up here and get to bed. I've got to go home early in the morning."

As he had promised, Scott Allison came to cradle the wheat when it was ready. George Blackburn and Mordecai and Bert Brown were there shortly after sunrise to help. Scott Allison was a fast hand in the wheat field with his light, tough cradle made of the buttress roots of an ash tree. He went swiftly down the field swinging the long-fingered cradle and laying the wheat to one side in even windrows. It kept Nat and Bert and the two men busy raking and binding and shocking behind him. Hannah went with Jack and Marty to watch for a short time. She would love to stay and help bind and stack the golden sheaves, but her place was in the house. She must have a good meal on the table for all the men at noon.

They finished the cradling and shocking just before sunset.

"You've got a good place here," Scott Allison said to Nat as he was leaving. "I hope you can keep it."

"If hard work will hold it, we'll keep it," said Nat.

"If there isn't too much rain, the wheat should be ready to thresh out in two weeks," Mordecai Brown told him. "I wouldn't carry too much to the threshing floor at one time. You waste less if you do it in small jags. Let us know if you need help."

"Thank you, sir," said Nat. "I think we can manage. Hannah is good help and the little ones do their share, too."

Hannah, as she drove Betsey into the barn, heard and smiled. She would go right in and fix Nat a good supper from the leftovers.

It was August before Hannah knew it. She thought often of Pa and Ma and little Sammie and had to keep her hands busy to keep the grief pushed out of her mind, but she was beginning to enjoy her role as housekeeper. She took pride in keeping the cabin clean and pleasant, she enjoyed cooking the meals that Nat and Jack so ravenously ate, she liked working in the garden with Jack and Marty.

The season was a lush one with plenty of rain, followed by warm, sunny days. The vegetables in the garden grew in abundance. It was a pleasure to work the loamy soil of the garden and bring in baskets full of tender green beans and yellow squash and great pods of okra. Jack and Marty fished in the little creek the other side of the wheat field, and Nat brought in plump young squirrels and rabbits for her to cook.

Occasionally Jane and Ephaniah Brown came to spend an afternoon and help with the mending. One afternoon when they came they brought two loaves of crusted white bread fresh from the oven and said they could stay for supper. Bert would ride over later to accompany them home.

"How very nice," Hannah said. The idea of playing hostess pleased her, and she knew Nat would be glad to see Bert. "Um-m-m, this bread smells good."

"That is Jane's first try," said Ephaniah, "and she wanted you to have part of it."

"Oh, goodie!" Marty sniffed at it appreciatively. "We made fresh butter this morning. That ought to be good with it."

"And Nat found a bee tree!" Jack squealed, jumping up and down. "We'll have white bread and honey."

"Honey really ought to go good with it," said Jane, pleased at the pleasure her gift had brought.

"Making white bread is something I haven't tried," said Hannah.

"Oh, we'll help you make a batch sometime," said Ephaniah. "Ma will give you some of her starter."

"I would like that," said Hannah. "Sometime after we thresh the wheat and have some flour ground."

They sat down to mending, visiting as they sewed, and a pleasurable peace settled over Hannah. It was nice to have friends like Jane and Ephaniah, better still to have a clean and pleasant home for friends to come to. There was two years' difference in Jane and Ephaniah's ages and Hannah came between them with Ephaniah a year older and Jane a year younger.

But they looked enough alike to be twins. They both had soft brown hair and eyes and clear, slightly freckled skin like their mother's.

After the mending was finished Hannah warmed the vegetables left over from dinner and fried the last of the cured ham that Mrs. Cambright had sent. Jane and Marty and Ephaniah set the table, sliced the bread and went to the springhouse for milk and butter. The frying ham filled the cabin with a savory aroma.

Nat and Bert came in after doing up the chores.

"Smells like some good cooking is going on here," said Bert. He was tall and dark-haired and pleasant-looking like his father.

"White bread!" exclaimed Nat. "Where did that come from?"

"Jane made it," Hannah told him. "And they are going to teach me as soon as we get some flour."

Nat grinned. "I knew there was a good reason for finding that bee tree."

It was a pleasant hour around the table. All the Browns were good company and Bert was a lively mimic. Jack was on his good behavior and Nat, so Hannah thought, was almost as good a host as Pa. It made her proud of him.

As they watched them ride off, Nat said, "I enjoyed that. I'm glad they came."

Hannah smiled. How many times she had heard

Pa say that very same thing to Ma after a pleasant visit with company. "Nat," she said, "does it seem to you— well—that—you love our home, the cabin and the farm better all the time?"

"Yes," said Nat, "I sure do."

"Oh, Nat. We've just got to keep it and stay together, somehow."

"Somehow we will, Hannah."

CHAPTER VIII

USUALLY HANNAH let Jack and Marty sleep mornings while she and Nat had breakfast. Nat would talk to her about the work on the farm the way Pa had always talked to Ma. It made Hannah feel grown up, indeed. Nat was proud of the corn crop. There had been plenty of rain at the right time, the stalks had grown high with a deep green color and the ears that set on were long and well filled out. The hay had been cut and stored in the barn before Joel left, the bean patch was in bloom, the late garden was thriving and the wheat in its plumed shocks was drying to a golden brown. Things were going well. If only little

Angie were near enough for them to see often. The Browns, no doubt, would lend her a horse to ride over to the Hopkins' if she asked them but Nat didn't want her to.

"Farmers need their horses this time of year," he had said when she mentioned it. "And when they are not using them, their women are. Besides, we shouldn't ask for any favors that we don't absolutely need. The neighbors have been good to us but we have got to prove that we can manage on our own, even without horses. As soon as I can, I will take a full day off from hunting and go over to see about little Angie."

"But I want to see her," Hannah complained.

"I know you do, Hannah," Nat said, and he sounded just like Pa comforting Ma. "Just as soon as there is a good heavy frost and the corn is gathered, we'll bring her home."

Hannah smiled. "Now that will be a real harvest."

When the wheat was thoroughly dried and ready for threshing, Hannah started rising before daylight every morning in order to get the necessary chores over as early as possible so that she could help long hours with the threshing Usually Nat would have the ox team hitched to the wagon and a load of sheaves hauled to the barn by the time she and Jack and Marty got out. They would carry the sheaves to the threshing floor and with long flails beat out the plump brown kernels from the slender stalks. When the floor was covered with grain, Nat would shake out the straw with a pitchfork and throw it to one side for Jack and Marty to stuff into gunnysacks and carry to the loft. Hannah would sweep up the grain and sack it. Then they would all carry in more fresh sheaves and start again.

Nat and Hannah put in long, steady hours, but Jack and Marty would grow tired of their job after a while and Hannah would tell them to run play. The second day, Nat made a swing for them by using one of the sacks filled with straw and tying one end of a long rope to the sack and the other end to a rafter by the loft door. They could grasp the rope, jump out the loft, land astride the straw-filled sack and sail through the air. It was so much fun that Nat and Hannah took a turn at it now and then. It was really great sport to scamper up the ladder, jump out the loft and go swinging out into the air.

When the wheat was all threshed, they loaded it into the wagon, keeping back plenty for seed wheat. Nat hitched the ox team to the wagon bright and early the next morning and started to Blue Mills with it, vowing that he would just as soon pull the wagon himself as to drive those creeping oxen.

"Yes, but think of all the biscuits we will have next winter out of the flour this wheat will make," Hannah reminded him

"They better be good," Nat grumbled.

Watching the oxen mosey off down the trail, Hannah thought that if there was a wagon track back to where the Hopkins lived, she would be tempted to put Jack and Marty in the wagon one day and drive those poky oxen over there to see little Angie.

"I can't bear it if we don't bring her home soon!"

The Hopkins lived back in the woods, everyone said, because Skip didn't like to farm. He preferred to hunt and trap and trade hides for necessities rather than to clear land and plant crops. The Hopkins had no near neighbors and there had been no word from little Angie since Joel left.

There was a warm, dry spell in September in which Hannah and Jack and Marty pulled the bean vines and shelled the dried beans while Nat broke the wheat patch with the ox team. When Nat had the soil thoroughly pulverized to make a good seedbed, they sowed it, carrying small bags of seed wheat under their arms.

"Now then," said Nat after they had finished, "all we need for a stand of wheat next spring is a good rain to bring it up before winter."

The dry spell was followed by heavy rains and an early frost. Nat, true to his word, made a hunting trip in the direction of the Hopkins' shack. He came back late in the afternoon with the word that little Angie was growing and happy.

"They seem to love her as much as if she were their own."

"Who wouldn't?" said Hannah.

"If this weather holds we will have the corn gathered before the middle of November," said Nat. "Then we will go after her."

CHAPTER IX

THEY ALL HELPED with the corn gathering. Hannah would get up before day and put the rabbits or squirrels in the big iron pot to simmer so that there would be stew when they came in at night. For their meal at noon, she filled a basket with cold meat and bread and butter which they ate beside the spring.

Hannah couldn't remember when she had enjoyed anything so much. The mornings and evenings were cool and brisk, the middle of the day pleasantly warm with an invigorating tang in the air. And all over the countryside there was a smoky blue haze that Mr. Washington Irving had written about when he visited Independence several years ago. Hannah would draw in a deep breath of the fresh, crisp air and feel that it was going to the bottom of her lungs. It gave them all a will to work and an appetite to go with it. When they came in at night they ate as they had never eaten before and went to bed to sleep the sound sleep brought on by a satisfying fatigue. Hannah noticed happily that Marty's thin little face was rounding out and becoming rosy.

Mordecai and Bert Brown and George Blackburn offered to help pick the corn but Nat refused.

"You have as much corn to pick as we have," he said. "Besides, there is no need of anyone doing anything for us that we can do for ourselves. We'll take some help at butchering time."

First they brought in all the pumpkins that had been planted in the corn, then they filled the rick south of the barn that Joel had put up before he left. Since they had no horses to take through the winter, Nat thought that they need not fill it more than two-thirds full. All of the rest he hauled to Sibley to put in Mr. Cambright's warehouse. Mr. Cambright would ship it down the river to St. Louis and sell it and keep the money for them until Joel returned. When the last load was in the warehouse Mr. Cambright said that they had at least eight hundred bushels to sell.

"And he says corn is bringing forty cents a bushel!" Nat told Hannah jubilantly.

On the day after they finished, Nat went to the

Browns' to borrow a horse for Hannah to ride to the Hopkins' to get little Angie. Nat thought that he should go but Hannah wouldn't hear to it.

"You don't know how to carry a baby in the saddle. Anyway, I want to go. Jack and Marty can spend the day with the Browns."

The Browns not only agreed to lend Nat a horse for Hannah but said that Ephaniah would ride along with her on another horse. It was too far for a girl to ride by herself, they said.

With Ephaniah going along for company, the day took on the air of a holiday. There had been a heavy frost that morning followed by a bright, warm sun in a cloudless sky. The woods was a riot of autumn color from the crimson of the sumac bushes to the gold and rust color of the maple trees.

"I have never seen a more wonderful day," Hannah declared.

"Couldn't be better," said Ephaniah. "I am glad the Hopkins live so far back in the woods. I could ride all day."

"I can't understand the Hopkins living way back here," said Hannah. "They never have cleared any land."

Ephaniah laughed. "Skip would rather hunt and trap than clear land and farm. Now I believe we turn off here and follow this other trail."

They came in sight of the Hopkins' shack with its sagging lean-to just before noon.

"Don't see any smoke," said Hannah.

"It is warm right now. Guess they don't need the heat."

"I would think that there would be some cooking going on at this time of day."

"I think Maggie just cooks when Skip brings in something from hunting," said Ephaniah.

As they rode up to the shack no sign of life appeared. There was no movement about the place, not even a dog.

"This is queer," said Ephaniah.

"Oh, dear!" said Hannah. "I hope they aren't gone today. It would be awful to ride way over here for nothing, and I wouldn't want to wait around here all day."

"I would hate to stay here all night." Ephaniah shuddered, looking at the dilapidated shack and the conglomerate mess of rags, hides, and dried potato peelings in the dooryard.

They called to the house but got no answer.

"Let's look around," said Hannah.

They got down, tied their horses, and went to the door, picking their way gingerly through the rubbish. The door, falling off the leather hinges, stood half ajar. Hannah knocked and called; when she got no answer, she pushed on the door. The door scraped on the dirt floor and stuck. She stepped in and looked around.

"Ephaniah! There is nothing here!"

"Nothing here? What do you mean?"

"I mean they aren't here. They are gone! Moved!"

"Moved?"

Ephaniah stepped in behind her and looked around. There wasn't a piece of furniture anywhere. Not a bench, chair, table, cradle or anything to show that anyone lived there, only a few rags and some broken crockery strewn about.

Hannah's face blanched. "They have moved and taken little Angie with them. Where—where do you suppose they have gone?"

"Oh, probably somewhere close about. They wouldn't go any distance without letting you know."

"I wouldn't be too sure of that," Hannah said hoarsely. "They wanted her awfully bad, but—but I didn't think they would run away with her."

"Oh, Hannah, I don't believe they have gone far."

"We should never have let them have her," Hannah moaned. "The shiftless moveabouts!"

"You didn't have much choice, Hannah. You know how babies raised on bottles are subject to summer complaint. Your Jersey cow's milk was giving her the colic, anyway. You couldn't have brought her through the summer."

Hannah shook her head despairingly. "I reckon I couldn't, but I sure do want her back now."

They waited awhile, then beat the brush in all directions, but the only signs they found were tracks toward the southwest. Exhausted and discouraged, they dropped on the ground to rest.

"How could they do this?" Hannah sobbed.

Ephaniah got to her feet. "Come on, let's go back and tell my pa. He and the neighbors will scout the countryside for the Hopkins. Likely as not Skip has found a place up on the Little Blue where he thinks he can do better with his winter trapping. He shouldn't be too hard to find."

"Maybe not, but they had no business going off with our little Angie."

It was mid-afternoon when Hannah and Ephaniah rode up to the Browns' cabin. Jack and Marty, followed by Lizzie and Jane and the younger children, rushed out to meet them.

"Where's the baby?" Jack shouted.

Hannah started to answer and burst into tears.

Ephaniah looked over the heads of the children, at her mother. "They've gone, Ma—cleared out bag and baggage and taken the baby with them."

Lizzie's hands flew up and her mouth formed a silent, horrified "O," then she whirled around to the children behind her.

"One of you boys run to the field and tell your pa to come right now."

The tired girls followed Lizzie into the kitchen and dropped down in the ladder-back chairs beside the hand-hewn walnut table. Jane brought boiled ham and cabbage and hominy from the cooking pots and poured out milk for them. Mordecai came in from the fields shortly.

"What do you think, Mr. Brown," said Lizzie almost before he was in the door. "Those Hopkins have pulled up stakes and left with little Angie."

"No! Not really!"

"Yes sir!"

"Well, I'll be doggoned!" Mordecai turned to Hannah and Ephaniah. "Couldn't it be that they have just gone somewhere in the neighborhood?"

"If they have, they have taken everything except for a few dirty rags and a broken crock."

"Well, surely somebody knows something of their whereabouts. I'll ride down to Sibley and over to Blue Mills and see if anyone has heard anything of them lately. You and the little ones stay here, Hannah. If I am not back before sunset, send word to Nat about what has happened."

Before dark, Lizzie sent Tom and Chris to tell Nat what had happened. He came as soon as he had finished the milking and feeding. Mordecai rode in right behind him.

"Well, there is one thing sure," Mordecai said as he strode in the door. "No one around Sibley or Blue Mills has seen anything of the Hopkins the last few weeks. Could be that they aren't far off, though. Skip likes good winter hunting. He could have moved over toward Lone Jack or more likely he could have moved up the Blue a piece."

"Well, we've got to find out," said Nat. "And right away."

"Yes. First thing in the morning I will round up a bunch of men to scout the country but we may be gone two or three days. Nat, I think you had better stay at home and look after things there."

"Hannah and the children could stay here, if Nat wants to go," said Lizzie. "I could send Tom and Chris with Hannah, night and morning, to do the chores."

Mordecai shook his head. "I think it might be better if he stayed. Look up your Indian friend, Nat. Do you know where he is?"

"There are two or three Indian winter camps between Blue Mills and the big springs around Independence. One of them is probably Sagameeshee's camp."

It wasn't necessary for Nat to hunt Sagameeshee. He was at their cabin door the next morning before they had finished breakfast. He came in clutching his blanket around him for it had turned cold in the night. He was wearing winter clothing, leggings that covered his legs and thighs, and a slipover hunting shirt made of softly dressed doeskin. For once he sat down at the table. Hannah brought him a bowl of hominy covered with milk, put the corn bread and sorghum by his plate.

"Hunting white man and squaw take your little one."

Hannah nearly dropped the coffeepot that she was bringing from the fire. It did beat all how Indians learned the news about white people.

"You know about our baby sister?" Nat said.

Sagameeshee grunted. "Go south."

"Oh, no! Oh, no!" Hannah cried. "Then we will never find her. They will just disappear."

Nat's jaw dropped. "How long ago?"

Sagameeshee hesitated. He could never count in English. "Maybe *nompa grehbenan* nights ago." An Indian never measured time in days. It was always in nights or sleeps.

Nat knew that *nompa* in Osage was two and *grehbenan* was ten. An Osage didn't count higher than ten. That meant two tens or twenty days ago. Nat's face darkened. "How did they go? By the Osage Trace?"

Sagameeshee grunted again, and nodded his head.

"Then that means they have gone down into Arkansas territory, probably."

There was no use asking an Indian how he knew or where he got his information but you could depend upon it that what he said was right. What was more,

Nat knew that Sagameeshee had come as soon as he knew that his news was correct. If the Hopkins had followed the Osage Trace into Arkansas, they could disappear back in those hills and nobody up here would ever hear of them again.

Nat pushed back his plate, his appetite gone, a dark and desperate look creeping over his face.

"I'd like to take a gun right now and go after them."

"You couldn't do that, Nat," Hannah protested, "with winter coming on. Besides, you would never find them."

Nat knew she was right, but the feeling of futility it gave him made him want to do something desperate. He pounded his fist on the table, jumped up and paced the floor.

"All the same I'd like to. And when I found them I think I'd bash Skip's head in."

"Nat, don't talk like that! They loved her, too."

"I don't care," Nat shouted, his face blazing. "She is our baby and they had no right to take her!"

Jack stared, wide-eyed and silent, and Marty sat crying softly and wiping her eyes on the sleeve of her linsey dress.

Sagameeshee alone continued to eat, ignoring the commotion his news had wrought. As soon as he had finished he got up and started out. At the door he stopped, looked back. "No look this winter. In spring maybe find." He went out the door and disappeared into the woods.

Hannah dropped into a chair. "I knew they wanted her, but I didn't dream that they would ever do a thing like this. They are gone and we will never lay eyes on them again."

The sorrow in Hannah's voice softened Nat's anger. He laid a comforting hand on her shoulder, spoke kindly. "Maybe it is like Sagameeshee said. Maybe in the spring we will find out something. The Indians have ways of learning things and Sagameeshee is our friend!"

"Yes, Sagameeshee is our friend, but can he do us any good—?"

"Well, Joel will be home in the spring. He will find a way, maybe. We'll do something. I promise you we will do something."

Hannah stared at the fire, said nothing. There was a knock at the door and Nat opened it to Mordecai Brown and Mr. Cambright. Their faces were serious.

"We met Sagameeshee in the woods. He told us about the Hopkins skipping out," said Mordecai. "If he is right, it would be like looking for a needle in a haystack."

"We know that," said Nat, his face grim.

Catching the stricken look on Hannah's face, Mordecai said gently, "I'm sorry, children, but I am afraid you will have to face it."

"There ought to be something we could do," said Nat.

"Just to be sure we have left no stone unturned," said Mr. Cambright, "the men of the neighborhood are going to scout the country for fifty miles around. But I fear the Indians are right."

"They usually are," Nat admitted reluctantly.

"Well, we had better be on our way. If there is anything we can do for you, Nat, all you have to do is say so."

"Thank you, sir."

For once Hannah didn't go with Nat to do the chores. Instead she stood and looked out the window, a paralyzing feeling of emptiness draining over her. The sound of Marty's sobbing drew her from the window. Jack, huddled on a stool in the chimney corner, was resting his elbows on his knees, his chin in his little hands. His large blue eyes were solemn, his mouth quivering. Hannah realized that she had more than her own sorrow to think of.

"We will just keep hoping," Hannah heard herself saying, just like Ma. "We won't give up hope. Maybe in the spring—well—anyway, we will do the best we can."

CHAPTER X

WINTER CLOSED IN RAPIDLY. Before the first heavy
snow fell, the Browns and the Blackburns came to
help with the butchering. They rendered lard outside
in the big black kettle. The women made sausage and
the men helped Nat to salt and hang the hams and
slabs of bacon in the smokehouse. After they had
dripped, Nat would make a slow fire of hickory chips
to smoke the meat.

Nat took a load of corn to Blue Mills and had
enough meal ground to last them through the winter.
He bagged a deer with his new rifle, dressed out the
meat with Mordecai Brown's help and traded the
hide for a keg of molasses.

"We are really fixed for winter," Hannah said proudly.

In January the weather turned bitterly cold. One morning when Nat came in with the milk he said there was a ring around the sun, surest sign in the world of falling weather.

"We are apt to have a snowstorm. I had better get up an extra supply of wood."

As soon as breakfast was over, Hannah wrapped up and went outside to help. With the two of them working and using the crosscut saw, they could saw a lot of wood. Later she bundled up Jack and Marty and had them carry it up close to the house and stack it by the door.

That night as she lay on the bed beside Marty, Hannah could hear the wind rising. She always thought of little Angie every time she woke in the night. During the day when she was busy, she did as Grandma Peabody had advised her and kept little Angie off her mind. But at night, if she woke, little Angie was the first thing she thought of. Where was she? Was she hungry? Every night before she got into bed, she would go to the bedroom window that faced south and look out. Under her breath she would whisper, "God, bring little Angie back to us."

It was snowing hard when Hannah got out of bed. Nat, after starting the fires, went to milk while Hannah got breakfast. Hannah shivered in the biting cold of the cabin as she stirred the fire and started breakfast. She had to break the ice in the water bucket to make coffee, and every egg in the cupboard was frozen. She wouldn't call Jack and Marty until the kitchen was warmer. She didn't want to risk Marty's taking cold.

Nat was gone so long that Hannah got uneasy. She scraped the frost from the kitchen window and looked out. She couldn't even see the barn. The snow was driving straight from the north on a high wind and piling up in drifts. Gracious! It had never taken Nat this long. Maybe she should go help him. She was just wrapping up to go when he came in, slamming the door behind him and leaning against it.

"This is awful. I'm frozen."

"What took you so long?"

"The dumb oxen. The pigs and the sheep and the cow were all inside but I had to hunt all over the pasture for those dumb brutes." He went to the fire and held out his hands, shivering.

Hannah quickly poured a cup of coffee for him and ladled up a bowl of steaming hominy.

Nat sat down by the fire, took the coffee, savoring its warmth.

"And where do you think I found them? Twenty feet from the barn lot by that clump of locusts."

"By the locusts?"

"It is that bad. I could scarcely see five feet away. Don't let the kids stick their heads out. We had better melt snow for water. There will be no getting to the spring today."

The snow fell all through the day. Toward evening the wind died down and gradually the snow slackened and dwindled off. During the night the sky cleared and the sun came up bright and glittering on a beautifully fantastic world. When she went to take warm water to the chickens, Hannah looked about. The barn, the smokehouse, the chickenhouse were all garbed in a clean white mantle. Every bush and tree was dressed in a lacy covering on which a million diamonds sparkled and danced in the sun. When she got back in the house Marty was tiptoeing at the window to see out above the frost on the lower part of the pane.

"It's just like fairyland," Marty gasped.

Nat came in. "Guess we better shovel some paths. This sun won't last. Pa always said when it cleared off in the night it wouldn't stay clear."

"We'll help! We'll help!" shouted Jack and Marty.

"It isn't as much fun as it looks," said Nat.

"Aw, Nat! We want to get out, too."

Hannah looked doubtful. "It is awfully tiresome, shut up in the house with nothing to do."

"Yes," said Marty. "We want to get out."

Hannah wrapped a comforter around Jack and buttoned his coat up around his ears. "Put on that old hug-me-tight of mine under your coat, Marty."

It took nearly two hours of hard work to shovel paths. They shoveled paths to the smokehouse and root cellar and another to the chickenhouse and on out to the barn. They had just finished and Hannah was cleaning off the shovels while Nat went up to open the loft door and pitch down hay for the oxen. Jack spied the sack swing that Nat had made last summer. He scrambled up the ladder to the loft, grabbed the rope and started to leap out the door.

"No! No!" Nat shouted. "That sack is ripped, Jack!"

But it was too late. Jack had already leaped out the door with the rope in his hand and landed astride the sack of straw. The sack split wide open and the straw fell out. Jack felt the sack go from under him, felt his body slip. He took one hand off the rope to clutch at the sack beneath him, dangled with one hand on the rope, struggled to grasp the rope again, lost his hold and fell in the path in front of the barn. Marty's screams brought Hannah running out of the barn. Jack, limp and white with the breath knocked out of him, lay, a crumpled heap, on the tunneled path between the two walls of snow.

"Are you hurt?" they all cried at once.

Nat picked him up and Jack gasped for breath and started to cry.

"At least he isn't killed," said Hannah.

Nat started to the cabin with Jack in his arms. "I

noticed that sack the other day. I knew it was worn out and I should have taken it down."

Hannah ran ahead and opened the door. "Put him in the rocker. You build up the fire and I'll take off his wraps."

At first Hannah thought he wasn't badly hurt, just a knot on his head and a bruise on the side of his face. Then she noticed that he couldn't raise his left foot. She rolled down his wool stocking, pushed up the red-flannel underwear and saw a swollen knot halfway between the knee and ankle. The leg was partially bent. She looked around at Nat, her face white as a sheet.

"Nat! His leg is broken."

Nat dropped the stick of firewood he had in his hand and came over to the rocker. Marty burst into tears and Jack started screaming.

"Will my leg come off? Will my leg come off?"

"No, no, honey. It isn't that bad." Hannah tried to comfort him, then turning to Nat she whispered, "Whatever shall we do?"

"Find somebody who can set it, that's what."

"Who? Could Sagameeshee's medicine man or Grandma Peabody set it?"

"I know who we'll get—that young doctor who has just come to Blue Mills."

"I can't remember that we ever had a doctor. Doctors cost money."

"Maybe the reason we never had a doctor was because there weren't any doctors out here."

There was a loud knock on the door and a hearty "hello." Mordecai Brown pushed open the door and stuck in his head.

"Just came over to see how you were faring in the storm, but I see you are all right. Plenty of wood up and paths shoveled—what's the matter?"

"Jack fell out of the loft and broke his leg."

Mordecai gave a low whistle. "I'll be dadburned." He came over to the rocker where Jack was crying and examined the leg. "I'm afraid he has."

"I'm going for the doctor," Nat said.

"No. I'll go. You go for my wife, Nat. First we'd better make him more comfortable. Draw up another chair to rest his leg on and bring some blankets."

Upon hearing the news Lizzie came as quickly as she could get there. When Mordecai arrived with the doctor she had big pieces of flannel and long strips of linen laid out for bandaging. Young Dr. Raymond, wearing a coon-skin cap and a buffalo-hide coat, came in carrying some short boards under his arm.

"Here, Nat, you and Mr. Brown make a box without a top and open at one end, about twice as wide as his leg. Well, young fellow," he said to Jack, "you are getting mighty daring leaping out of barn lofts."

Jack stopped his whimpering and grinned, but he yelled when Dr. Raymond grasped his leg firmly and set the bone together and wrapped his leg in the strips of linen that Lizzie provided.

"That's tough, young fellow, but it's something we had to go through. Now we will put him in a comfortable spot where we will keep him for a while."

Hannah went into the bedroom and turned back the covers on Ma and Pa's bed. Dr. Raymond picked up Jack and carried him to the bedroom and had Hannah prop him up with pillows.

"Now bring the box."

He lined the box with a big piece of flannel that Lizzie brought, then told them to bring either sand, bran, or cornmeal. Hannah went to the cupboard and brought back a crock full of meal. This Dr. Raymond put in the lined box to form a cushion for the foot and lower part of the leg. After that he secured Jack's foot to the foot board with strips of linen.

"Just keep him quiet and entertain him. I'll give him a little laudanum to make him rest."

As Dr. Raymond picked up his things to leave Nat said, "We don't have any money to pay you, Dr. Raymond, but I think Mr. Cambright will let us have enough to pay you out of the money he got from the corn he shipped down the river for us."

"Thank you, Nat, but I am not the kind of man to take money for a service to a bunch of brave kids. I am glad to help you."

"We appreciate it, Doctor, but we are not the kind

to take something for nothing," Nat said. "We've got to make our own way."

Dr. Raymond smiled. "You are quite a man, Nat."

And Hannah felt a surge of pride that amounted almost to happiness in the midst of all this calamity.

"I'll tell you what, Nat. In that fine big barn you must have plenty of hay. Sometime when you are going to Blue Mills bring me a load of hay."

"That will be fine. You shall have it as soon as the wagon road is open."

"I will stop in now and then when I am over this way. Should you need me, send for me."

Lizzie Brown spent two days with them and would have stayed longer but Bert came with word that Chris was sick.

"I hate to leave you," said Lizzie. "I'll come back as soon as I can."

"Oh, we'll make out," said Hannah, but inwardly she felt that something had dropped from beneath her. Having Lizzie was almost like having Ma to depend on.

As Nat predicted, the sun disappeared, the sky turned gray and the clouds hung low. There was no more snow but the cold hung on and the next few days were as dark and gloomy as Hannah had ever seen. Jack was restless and fretful, demanding attention every minute. He kept Hannah and Marty on the run all day long. Nat did all the outside chores, looked after the stock and kept the fires going. The second night after Lizzie left, Hannah was so nearly exhausted that she thought when she sank down in the feather bed beside Marty she would never be able to rise again. But it was not long until Jack called her.

"My back aches, Hannah."

Hannah got up to turn his pillows and make him as comfortable as she could. While she was up she put more wood on the fire. It was then that she noticed Marty's breathing was labored. Presently she began to wheeze.

"Marty," Hannah called softly. "Are you all right?"

Marty made a suffocating sound, accompanied by more wheezing. Fear clutched Hannah anew. That was croup and no mistake. Hannah went into the kitchen, lighted a candle and, careful not to wake Nat, looked in the medicine chest for the dried mullein leaves that Ma always used to make a vapor when one of the children had croup. She put another log on the kitchen fire and swung the kettle over it. As soon as the water boiled she poured it over the mullein leaves and put it on a chair by Marty's side of the bed. Then she went to the kitchen to make a flaxseed poultice. She stirred the flaxseed into the boiling water until it thickened, then added a little olive oil and spread it on a cloth the way Ma used to do. As soon as it had cooled a little, she took the poultice into the bedroom and laid it across Marty's throat.

"Here, honey," she said, using Ma's tone of voice. "Maybe this will make you feel better."

The wheezing persisted. Marty coughed, raised her head and sounded as if she were choking. Hannah raised Marty up in bed.

"Can't you bring up the phlegm, Marty? Try."

Marty raised her head, made a sound in her throat and dropped back on her pillow. Hannah turned her on her side, shoved another pillow under her head and ran to call Nat.

"Nat, Nat!" she called. "Get up. Marty's got the croup—bad."

"Huh? What?" Nat said, rising up from his bed by the fire and rubbing his eyes. "What did you say?"

Old Zip, sleeping at Nat's feet, jumped up and whined.

"Marty's got the croup—bad. Get up and build up the fire and put more water in the teakettle."

Nat jumped up and started stirring the fire.

Hannah went back to the medicine chest, took out two grains of tartar emetic and poured over it syrup of ipecacuanha as she had seen Ma do. To this she added a little hot water and took it to the bedroom.

"Here, Nat. You help me hold her up and keep the blanket around her so she won't catch any more cold."

"Hannah—Hannah—" Jack called, but for once she paid no attention to him.

Hannah held the warm emetic to Marty's lips.

Marty took some but without any result. Hannah gave her a little more but still the phlegm didn't come up.

Hannah waited a few minutes. "Bring some more warm water, Nat."

Nat brought the water and Hannah added another grain of tartar emetic. She held it to Marty's lips. Marty swallowed, gasped, gagged, and the phlegm came up. Hannah gave a long, shuddering sigh of relief, and carried the bowl and medicine back to the kitchen. Nat built up the fires in both rooms and went back to bed. Hannah took away the mullein water that had grown cold, poured more boiling water over fresh leaves and put it back beside Marty and crawled into bed.

Hannah knew it was late in the morning when she woke, even though there was no sun and the sky was a lead gray. Wearily she pulled herself out of bed and dressed. Nat had gone out to do the chores and the small fire that he had built in the fireplace had burned down leaving the kitchen cold and cheerless. As low as the clouds hung, any kind of weather could come out of them—snow, sleet, wind—anything. With a heaviness that bore down on her spirits, Hannah stirred up the fire and started breakfast. Jack woke, crying out in pain. She went into the bedroom, built up the fire and rubbed Jack's leg and his back. Marty was awake but lying still with her eyes half closed.

She wasn't coughing or wheezing but her cheeks were flushed with fever.

Nat came in stamping his feet and blowing on his fingers. Hannah put hot mush and coffee and strips of bacon on the table for him. Before she sat down she took Jack's breakfast to him, but Marty refused food.

Morning dragged into afternoon. Hannah knew that in all her life she had never been so tired. She was weary in mind, body and soul. So much had happened to them. Was there no end? Between taking care of Marty and waiting on Jack she had had no time for housekeeping. The floors were unswept, the hearth and pine table unscrubbed, dust lay on all the furniture, everything had an unkempt look to it. Nat was doing everything on the outside, even to melting snow for water and feeding the chickens, but, even so, she couldn't keep up with all there was to do.

She found no time for cooking at noon, just warmed over the cornmeal mush. Nat didn't complain, although Hannah knew he was hungry.

But Jack complained. "I don't want it. We had mush for breakfast."

Marty tried to eat a few bites but had a hard time swallowing. Her face was flushed with fever and she couldn't speak above a whisper.

"Do you think I should go for the doctor?" Nat asked.

"I don't know," Hannah said wearily. "Ma always doctored us when we were sick and we got along all right." Hannah looked out at the lead-gray sky. "Maybe you should but it sure looks like another storm is brewing. I think I would go crazy if you got caught out in a storm. Anyone could get lost in one like we had the other day."

As she stood looking out the window a feeling of desperation spread over her, her throat knotted and her eyes filled. She tried to speak, opened her mouth, then held it open. Someone was riding out of the woods, someone bundled from head to foot and sitting on a side saddle. Could it be? Was it possible? It was —Grandma Peabody!

"Nat! Nat! Here's Grandma Peabody!"

Hannah dashed out the door without coat or cap, Nat right on her heels.

"Grandma! Grandma!"

"Laws a' massy! Children, help me unload this horse."

She had the saddlebags full and behind her was a tiny trunk strapped to the horse's back. Nat led the horse up to the stile and Grandma climbed down.

Hannah threw her arms around the little old lady, laughing and crying at the same time.

"Grandma! Grandma!"

"Get yourself back in the house, girl, before you take your death of cold," Grandma ordered. "And you too, Nat. Put on your wraps before you take my horse around to the barn."

Hannah led the way into the cabin and drew up a chair in front of the fire.

Jack, waking from a nap, shouted, "Who's here? Who's here?"

"Hush up, Jack," Grandma ordered. "I'll see you in a minute."

"Oh, it's Grandma Peabody! Goodie!"

"How did you ever happen to come out in this weather?"

"Shucks. I've been out in worse. I think another storm is brewing, though, and I thought I would get over here ahead of it. I've been intending to come back to help you get some sewing and weaving done. Then when Mordecai Brown came over and told me about Jack, I just put my clothes in my little trunk and started."

"Oh, Grandma, this is wonderful. How long can you stay?"

"As long as you need me. I had my nephew Hezekiah come get my cow. With their big family they can use the extra milk. The neighbors across the road will look after my chickens and gather the eggs. Here now, help me get my clothes unpacked."

After she had seen Marty they asked Grandma if Nat should go for the doctor. Grandma pooh-poohed the idea.

"A doctor can't do any more for her than I can. My saddlebags are full of medicine—medicine made from herbs that I gathered or Sagameeshee brought me. No guesswork about it. All these doctors know is bleeding and purging and a lot of Latin words. They could learn more by listening to the Indians. She's got quinsy. On top of croup that's made her pretty sick. She will be all right in a few days. Bring me some turpentine and lard. I'm going to grease her chest and put a warm flannel on it. That will loosen up her cold in no time. We'll keep the mullein vapor going again tonight so that she won't choke up."

Grandma admitted grudgingly that the young doctor's idea of putting Jack's leg in a box with meal packed around it did make sense.

"It does stand to reason that the leg is more comfortable that way, but there is no sense in keeping him in bed all the time. No wonder he is so restless. We can bring him into the kitchen and fix him up comfortably in the rocker with a block of wood under it to keep it from moving. Then we can put his boxed leg on a straight chair. If we keep him in here during the day he won't get so tired of the bed at night."

"I'm sorry for you to find our cabin so untidy, Grandma," Hannah apologized.

"First things come first. We'll get it all tidied up tomorrow. And now," she said, tying an apron over her linsey-woolsey dress, "you get out and help Nat with the evening chores while I get supper. It's going to get dark early. While you are out, bring up some lard from the cave. A pan of hot biscuits ought to go good."

"We got plenty of flour in the smokehouse," Nat said proudly. "Close to two hundred pounds."

"Fine. Sounds like you are a good provider, Nat. I brought a little jar of quince jelly."

"Quince jelly!"

"Why, Grandma!" Hannah cried. "We never had jelly except when we had special company."

"There are times when you need a special treat, and right now is the time to have hot biscuits and jelly. Bring up a batch of potatoes before you milk. I want to make potato soup for Marty. And while you are in the cellar you might as well bring up turnips and hominy, too. With a storm moving in, we might as well lay in some vittles."

"All right," said Nat, "and I'll get cabbage and parsnips from the pit. Shall I bring in a piece of shoulder meat?"

"If you've got plenty, why not? Law me! We will live like kings while the storm is on."

CHAPTER XI

THE STORM lasted three days and when it was over they were completely snowed in except for the paths Nat and Hannah kept shoveled. But this time Hannah didn't worry. On the contrary, it gave her a pleasurable feeling. Marty was improving and Jack wasn't so restless. All the time she and Nat were shoveling paths or doing up chores in the cold she was thinking about the good hot meal Grandma would have for them and the pleasant things they would do afterwards.

Marty was up in less than a week, and Grandma had Jack, as well as Marty, knitting. Jack caught on rapidly and when Nat, at Hannah's nudging, praised his work he tried all the harder.

"He is better satisfied if he is busy," Hannah whispered. "Don't let him think it's sissy."

Grandma found the old blue-back speller and taught him to spell a few words and read a little.

"Next year you must send Jack and Marty to the subscription school. Your mother saw to it that you older ones had some schooling and they must, too."

Mr. and Mrs. Cambright drove over in a sleigh and brought a basket of apples and a book of Washington Irving's stories. Alice Blackburn sent gingerbread and a fluffy yellow kitten that delighted Jack and Marty.

"We are doing well on our misfortunes." Hannah laughed. "We are having a feast every day."

Grandma had brought hand-loomed linsey-woolsey cloth to make shirts for Jack and Nat and a dress each for Hannah and Marty. She found some carded wool in the attic, threaded the spinning wheel and showed Hannah how to adjust the tension, and Hannah set to work spinning while Grandma sat in the loom.

The noise of the busy routines made a pleasant sound in Hannah's ears. Grandma worked the treadle of the loom with her foot and threw the shuttle and snapped the reed with her hands. As Hannah worked the treadle of the spinning wheel with her foot and guided the wool with her free hand, watching the yarn wind evenly on the spool, a sense of security settled over her. There were hams and bacon in the smoke-house, parsnips and cabbage in the cellar, corn in the rick and flour in the cupboard, and every bit of it from their summer's work. With the fresh meat Nat brought in now and then, they were living sumptuously. Seemed as if it just took Grandma and her way of settling everyone down to pleasant winter work to make her realize it. If only Joel was back and little Angie was toddling around. Well, Joel would be back in the spring, Hannah told herself firmly, and maybe he would know of some way to get little Angie back.

Grandma didn't believe in working after supper.

"Days should be busy," she said, "but your work should lead up to something pleasant in the evening."

She taught them guessing games, she made a checkerboard and had Nat bring in red and yellow grains of corn for checkers, and twice they had a molasses taffy pull that all the Browns came to. She read aloud the *Legend of Sleepy Hollow* and *Rip Van Winkle* and on Sundays she read from the Bible.

But best of all they loved her stories. She told stories of Indian raids back in Kentucky or stories of early days in the Boone's Lick country when she and her husband first came there. There was a big bee hunt that she mentioned frequently.

"Men came for miles," she said, "as far as St. Charles, even. Forty wagons left Franklin with four men to a wagon. They spent a month at the headwaters of the Chariton and Grand. Every man struck out for himself and when he found a bee tree he would carve his initials on it, and a man who would cut down a tree with another man's initials on it was no better than a thief. When they came back, all the wagons were loaded with honey."

"What did they do with it?"

"Ate some of it, of course. After the honey was pressed out we used the beeswax for money."

"Money?" They all shouted and laughed at the idea.

"Oh, pshaw! Since the Mexican trade started between Independence and Santa Fe you young'uns haven't heard of anything but Spanish bits and dollars. We didn't have any dollars so we had to use something for currency. Beeswax cakes were called 'yellow boys' and passed for twenty-five cents a pound. Once in a while someone would counterfeit and offer a beeswax cake with a tallow filling, but a man who would do a thing like that was always shunned by his neighbors."

"But you couldn't eat all that honey "

"No, in fact, very little. It was too valuable. We shipped most of it to St. Louis. If I rightly remember, that big bee hunt brought in thirty-nine hundred dollars in gold."

"Wow!" Nat slapped his knee. "Looks like I better start hunting bee trees."

With Grandma there with Jack and the girls, Nat

would run his trap lines and hunt for long stretches of time, coming in sometimes after dark.

"It's a sure shot," he would say pridefully of his rifle. "There isn't much game now but if I ever see a rabbit this gun can take the eye right out of it."

After he had brought in a few skins, he would build a fire in the smokehouse and spend hours dressing and curing the hides. One evening as Nat came around the barn whistling with two beavers and a possum over his shoulder, Hannah, who had just finished the chores by herself, came out of the barn with the milkpail on her arm.

"Well, Mr. Gadabout, you've stayed out again until the chores are all done."

"Why, Hannah," he said, "don't you know why I am dressing out these hides?"

"No, I don't," Hannah snapped.

"Hannah, we don't know how much Joel will bring back. Maybe he will bring back enough to pay the debt and maybe he won't. One thing sure, old Baxter won't show us any mercy. Hunting or trapping isn't good this winter. It's been so cold that a lot of the game has starved or moved south, but if I stay with it, I can get a little. Mr. Cambright will take every skin that I get a good cure on. With luck I might bring in twenty-five or thirty dollars."

"I'm sorry, Nat. I thought you were just having a good time with your fine rifle."

"Well, I reckon that is part of it, but I do aim to

have hides to sell if I can find them. I guess it does work you pretty hard doing the housework and the outside chores, too."

"Not with Grandma here. I'll do the chores mornings, too, Nat, if you want to get out early."

"You are a good girl, Hannah, and a lot of help."

Hannah smiled. To think that a year ago he was pulling her hair and calling her a blunderbuss.

When they told Grandma she nodded her approval.

"Good idea. Don't depend on the other person for everything. Do what you can yourself. If Joel brings home enough to pay off the mortgage—fine. If he doesn't, your skins will help out. I can stay until April and you can spend as much time hunting as you like."

There was intermittent snow all through February and March but no more big storms. The severe cold held on, though. Game was scarce. Sometimes Nat would spend a whole day in the woods and come in with one skinny rabbit or a tough squirrel. It was a bleak, raw day early in March, but in the cabin the fire leaped cheerfully as Grandma stirred it to heat the brick oven. They had peeled a pumpkin the night before—their last one—and Grandma had cooked it, sweetened it with sorghum and made it into pies. Hannah hummed a tune as her foot worked the treadle of the spinning wheel.

Dr. Raymond had just left after unbinding Jack's

leg. Jack had walked fearfully and cried with the pain but Dr. Raymond was reassuring. "That is natural. It will take a few days. After that he will walk as well as ever."

Grandma had just put the pies in the oven when the door opened and Sagameeshee stalked in, sniffing at the smells that came from the cooking pots. He was pleased to see his friend Grandma Peabody here, managed what amounted almost to a smile in answer to Grandma's banter.

"It's about time you were showing up. Haven't seen hide nor hair of you since last fall. I want you to bring me some hemlock bark to mix with golden seal and Osage orange. I need it to make up dyes for my yarn."

"Nat's in the barn stretching hides," Hannah told him. But Sagameeshee, attracted by the smell of the cooking, made no move to leave.

When Nat came in, he was pleased to see his friend but Sagameeshee was even less inclined to talk than usual. Hannah set a great bowl of food in front of him, large pieces of ham cooked with potatoes and beans, and Sagameeshee started spooning it up gustily. Best of all he liked the corn bread. He took the last piece, then scraped up the crumbs. After eating the big wedge of pie Grandma set in front of him, Sagameeshee took out his pipe and smoked.

"Sagameeshee," Nat said, "have you had any word from up the river?"

Hannah stopped the spinning wheel to listen. She knew that Nat was thinking about the trading party Joel was in. What Sagameeshee said then Hannah had reason to recall later.

"Sioux, Blackfeet—bad medicine." More than that he would not say.

"Gracious!" said Grandma after Nat and Sagameeshee had gone to the barn. "He ate like he was starved."

After while Nat, with Sagameeshee behind him, came in and spoke directly to Hannah. "Sagameeshee and his friends on the other side of the Blue aren't faring well this winter."

"The Osage never fare well in a long winter," Grandma said sadly. "They just don't farm enough to raise corn to do them, and unless there is lots of game at this time of year they go hungry."

"In Sagameeshee's camp they are worse off than the other Osage. There aren't many young men in his camp and the hunting has been poor. Hannah," Nat said, "don't you think we can spare them some of our corn and a few slabs of bacon?"

It pleased Hannah that Nat had come in to consult her, just like Pa always talked everything over with Ma. "If we have it to spare, Nat, I don't see why not."

"It isn't so much that we have it to spare, in fact it will pinch us if we let them have enough to do any good. It hurts an Indian to know that his children are hungry just the same as it hurts a white man to see his children hungry."

"I'm sure of it," said Hannah. "But I was just wondering if we might give something and ask the Browns and the Blackburns and the Cambrights to give something."

"You know what Pa always said about that, Hannah. He said not to ask someone else to do a good deed that you can do yourself. Besides, Sagameeshee is our friend, not their friend."

"Let them have as much as you want to, Nat," Hannah said. "I think you are doing right."

Grandma beamed on all of them. "You are good children."

"Come on, Sagameeshee, you take home a sack of corn and some slabs of bacon, then send your young men and I will give them *taupa grehbenan* bushels of corn," Nat said, holding up his ten fingers four times.

Sagameeshee's jaw dropped in amazement. *"Taupa grehbenan?"*

"That's what I said—four tens, forty bushels. It will take that much to carry you over till warm weather."

A light leaped up in Sagameeshee's eyes. "You do this for my people, young friend?"

"Of course."

"Sagameeshee and his people do not forget."

CHAPTER XII

GRANDMA LEFT in April but not until after she had supervised the shearing and washing of the wool. Early one morning she gathered up her belongings, put her clothes in the tiny trunk and gave orders until she got on her horse.

"Remember to plant your corn in the light of the moon when the sign is in the arms, and sow your turnips in the dark of the moon. All of you drink your sassafras tea and get your wool carded before the heavy summer work starts."

They stood in the dooryard and watched her ride off through the flowering dogwood and the budding elms and maples.

"Now, then," said Hannah, "I think we can start looking for Joel before long."

"And when he comes, I will have a good start on the plowing," said Nat.

Each morning when Hannah got up, she thought, "Now Joel will come today." She kept the cabin as tidy as possible and kept food in the cooking pot even though she was working in the garden a great deal of the time now. There must be a good homecoming for Joel. Unless it rained, Nat was in the field from sunup till dark.

April with its warm showers passed into the balminess of May. The creek banks were full of violets and wild greens grew in abundance. Frogs struck up a concert at dusk and the whippoorwills called in the woods but Joel didn't come.

George Blackburn and Bert Brown brought teams to finish the plowing and Mr. Cambright sent a man to help plant, so that Nat could get the corn crop in early.

"I wish we could have done it all by ourselves," said Nat. "But with Joel not here and only the ox team I just couldn't get it done."

"I only hope we aren't getting it done for old Gideon Baxter. He rode by the cabin today."

"Oh, he did?"

"Yes, he even talked rather nice. Said we had things in good shape. Seemed surprised that we had managed so well."

"Reckon he thinks it will be in good shape to take over," Nat snorted. "Mr. Cambright says the probate period will be over in June. Wish Joel would hurry up and come."

"Nat, are you worried about Joel? I mean do you think that, well, that Joel might not get back?"

Nat hesitated. "Yes, Hannah. I've thought about it a lot. In fact it has begun to worry me more than the prospect of losing this place."

"It has me, too, Nat. I just wonder what is going to happen next."

"I don't know," Nat admitted dismally. "Yet I just can't find it in me to give up. I just have to go on plowing and working and hoping."

"Have you seen Sagameeshee lately? Sometimes Indians get word from up the river."

Nat shook his head. "Can't find him. His squaw, Pokaleeta, isn't there either. The others just say he is gone. You can't get anything out of an Indian unless he wants to talk."

It rained that night, and the next day was too wet for work in the fields. Nat was so restless that Hannah was glad when he said he was going to the Browns'.

"Give me a pail. If Bert isn't busy maybe we will go out and find a bee tree."

He came back before dark with a pail full of light amber chunks of honey.

"This calls for hot biscuits," said Hannah.

They hadn't had any honey in months. They all enjoyed it so much that there was an almost cheerful air around the supper table. After supper Hannah mentioned the matter of supplies to Nat.

"We've used the last of the bacon and I should be stretching out the flour, but we are low on cornmeal, too. I'm not sorry we helped the Indians, though."

"They would have gone awfully hungry if we hadn't. Game is getting more plentiful. I will go out first thing in the morning and get some young squirrels."

The next day was still too wet to work in the fields, but the sun came out bright.

"Today was sure made for working out-of-doors," Hannah said, "but the ground is too wet to work."

"I know something we can do," said Nat. "Make bee gums."

"Bee gums?"

"I've heard Pa tell about making bee gums out of hollow logs when he was a boy."

"But what for? Can't you go to the woods and find a bee tree when you want it?"

"Sometimes. But a farmer is usually busy at the time honey is at its best and hasn't time to look for honey. Anyway, wild honey is like game. As more people move out here, it becomes more scarce."

"You mean we could have bees on the place and have honey whenever we want it?"

"Not only that, but you heard what Grandma Peabody said about shipping honey down the river. If we had gums, we could build up a colony of bees and sell honey."

"Nat! That sounds wonderful!"

"It's worth trying and it is one thing we could take with us if we have to leave this place."

Hannah's face fell. "But if we are divided up and sent to other homes—"

Nat scowled. "I'm not going to think about that. As soon as the chores are done, I'll go see if Bert Brown can help me cut down some hollow trees."

"Go right now. The kids and I can do the chores."

With Bert's help Nat cut and trimmed two hollow trees. Jack and Hannah had the oxen hitched to the sled when Nat came out of the woods. After they had hauled the felled trees to a shaded spot east of the cabin, Nat and Hannah sawed them into three-foot sections and set them on blocks of oak. Nat whittled rods from hickory saplings to run through the centers for the bees to build their comb on. There was a small stack of shakes in the barn left over from roofing the chickenhouse. These they used to make tops. Jack and Marty brought moss from the creek to cover the roofs. That would keep them warm in winter and cool in summer.

It was late in the afternoon and they were almost finished when Mr. Cambright rode up.

"What are you kids doing?"

"Making bee gums," said Nat.

"Bee gums! First time I ever heard of them in this part of the country. What do you plan to do with them?"

"I'm going to fix up a smoke pot, and all the time I can spare out of the field I'll hunt bees that are swarming. I can smoke them until they are numb, saw off the limb they settle on and bring them in."

"Aren't you figuring on eating quite a lot of honey?"

"No, sir. I want to sell it. I hear there is a market for it. Don't you buy it and ship it to St. Louis?"

"I do when I can get it. Hasn't been much brought in the last year or two."

"How much does it sell for?"

"All the way from one bit to three bits a gallon, depending on the quality and the supply. Right now it is high. The last I shipped brought thirty-seven and a half cents a gallon."

"Well, I intend to have some to sell before the end of the summer. If Baxter turns us out of this place, we can take the hives with us."

"Nat, you've got a mighty level head on your shoulders."

"Thank you, sir."

"Mr. Cambright," said Hannah, "have you had any word about Joel and his party?"

Mr. Cambright hesitated. Nat looked up sharply

and Jack and Marty came to stand by the horse, searching his face for the answer.

"There has been trouble with the Indians this winter—the Sioux, the Otoes and the Blackfeet, in particular. Nothing is known for certain, only that Roubeau's party left Fort Union later than the others, probably around the first of April. Chouteau's party passed through here three weeks ago. He thought Roubeau would follow him shortly. Nothing has been heard of them since."

Hannah's face blanched. She clenched her hands and knotted her shoulders to keep from shaking, but Nat, she noticed, was standing straight and unquivering, his face solemn, his jaw set.

CHAPTER XIII

IN THE DAYS that followed, Hannah felt that she had just become hands and feet going about the daily routine of chores, a weight dragging at her heart. The garden thrived, the corn grew and the wheat was a beautiful sight to behold, but Hannah drew no pleasure from looking at it. Each morning she expected Gideon Baxter to ride up, demand payment and order them out.

For last year's corn crop they had received two hundred and sixty dollars after freight charges and their bill for supplies were paid. This Mr. Cambright was keeping for them along with twenty-seven dollars for hides Nat had brought in. That wasn't nearly enough. Had Joel come back with the four hundred dollars he had expected, they could have paid off the mortgage. As it was now, they didn't have the money. Worse still, they didn't have Joel or little Angie.

Late in the afternoon on the first day of June, Mr. Cambright sent word that Gideon Baxter would be at his store early the next afternoon and Nat was to come down to see him.

"I suppose that is to tell us he is taking our place away from us."

"And parcel us out," Hannah added in a stricken voice.

The next morning at breakfast Hannah told Nat she wanted to go with him.

"I think I couldn't bear to wait here for you to come tell me."

"I don't know why you shouldn't go. You've worked as hard as I have to hold this place."

"We'll go right after dinner. Jack and Marty can stop off at the Browns'."

Hannah kept as busy as she could to keep her mind off what was in front of them. She cleaned the cabin and fixed the churn for Jack and Marty to make butter. She gathered wild greens and put them on to cook with ham and new turnips. She sent Jack and Marty to the garden for green peas. While they were doing that she picked blackberries.

Before she put the corn bread in the oven, Hannah went to call Jack and Marty in to wash and change clothes. As she stepped outside the door, she saw a man come out of the woods and start across the meadow. He walked with a long stride and was dressed like an Indian but his hair was long, almost to his shoulders. It wasn't any of the neighbors. He was in the clearing before she recognized him.

"Joel! Joel!" she screamed, and ran to meet him. "Jack, Marty! Call Nat! Joel's home."

Her shouts brought Jack and Marty tearing around the cabin and their clamor brought Nat on the run from the barn. Joel scooped up Jack and set him on his shoulder and threw an arm around Marty.

"Gee, kids. It's great to see you again. Nat, you've grown a foot."

Nat pounded him on the back. "It's great to see you."

"Great!" said Hannah. "That doesn't begin to say it, especially when—when we thought—" To her dismay she was crying.

Joel swung out his free arm and drew her to him. "U-u-mm," he said. "I smell cooking."

"Oh," said Hannah, drying her eyes on the corner of her apron and becoming the housekeeper again. "I've got to get my corn bread in. Dinner is almost ready."

"First," said Joel, "I want to burn these rags and

scrub and put on clean clothes. I hope I have some."

"You sure have," said Hannah going to the chest and bringing out a pair of neatly mended homespun jeans and a hickory shirt.

Before they sat down to the table, they told him about the Hopkins going off with little Angie and the Indians taking their horses.

Joel's face darkened. "We can get other horses— but the baby. Well, as soon as I can, I'll strike out to look for her. Do you suppose Sagameeshee has heard any more about the Hopkins?"

"I haven't seen Sagameeshee in a long time. I don't know where he is."

Hannah thought that she had never seen anyone eat like Joel did, not even Sagameeshee.

"What a fine cook you have turned out to be, Hannah," he said, refilling his plate and taking a third wedge of corn bread. "We didn't take out much time for hunting or cooking on the way back. Just ate a little jerked venison that the Pawnees gave us."

"Why didn't Mr. Roubeau visit us again?" Marty asked.

"He stopped in Sibley. He wanted to see Mr. Cambright. A steamboat is leaving for St. Louis early in the morning. He wants to take it."

"What will he do with the hides and the other men?" Nat asked.

"There were no hides and no other men."

"No hides? No other men?"

Joel nodded. "That's right. We lost all our hides. We were lucky to get away with our hair. In fact, Pierre Roubeau and I were the only ones who did."

"You mean you fought the Indians?" Jack said, his eyes as big as saucers.

Joel laughed shortly. "You might say that. At any rate, there was a skirmish and we came out second best."

"Then you—you—you haven't *any* hides?" Nat said incredulously.

Hannah's mouth flew open. A look of consternation spread over Nat's face.

"That's right." Joel spoke solemnly. "Not one hide did I bring back. Only my hair."

Nat, ashamed of the disappointment he had shown, tried to speak cheerfully. "That's all right, Joel. We are all thankful you got back."

"Indeed we are," Hannah seconded him.

"It isn't all right," said Joel, "but we will have to make the best of it."

"Mr. Cambright sent word for me to come down this afternoon. Gideon Baxter is going to be there."

"I know. I came by way of Sibley. I talked to Mr. Cambright. You did all right on your part, Nat—two hundred and eighty-seven dollars—but we need four hundred more."

"Tell us about your trip," said Hannah.

"Well," said Joel, "we reached Fort Union in September and spent the winter at the mouth of the Yellowstone River. Hunting was good and the season lasted later than usual. By the end of March I had four bales of prime skins for my share that Roubeau said should bring me around six hundred dollars. We left the Mandan villages on the last day of March and started down the river. We were heavily loaded and the going was slow. Except for an occasional scout we saw no Indians after we passed the Oto villages, but Roubeau was careful. He was sure a trader ahead of us had sold guns to the Otoes, although that is forbidden by the government. He tied up early every night and set two men at each watch. Not until we passed Fort Tecumseh did he appear to be easy.

"Then it happened. We weren't quite sure but Roubeau thought that the guards on second watch fell asleep. There was a sudden wild cry and all at once there was a swarm of Indians on the boats and on the shore. Before we were thoroughly awake, half of our men were dead, and before the rest of us could lay hands on our guns, they had killed several more and set fire to the boats, grabbed up all the guns and powder they could snatch and were off. Roubeau and I got in our licks. We brought down two before they got away. Well, to make a long story short—when it was over, Roubeau and I were the only ones left. The only reason they didn't stay and wipe us out is the

Indian fear of being killed in the night. They think if they are killed in the night their souls will not rest. They got what guns and ammunition they could and got away fast.

"We took out overland and hid in a thicket all day, afraid that they might come back after us. It probably was a bunch of young Sioux sent out to round up guns and ammunition to use on their old enemies, the Otoes. Roubeau thought that when the Sioux learned a trader had sold guns to the Otoes, it made the Sioux furious and they had sent out a party to get the guns and ammunition of any white trader they could find.

"All the other hunting parties had gone down the river ahead of us so that there was no chance of joining up with another party. We started walking and on the fourth day Roubeau stepped in a hole and sprained his ankle. By the next day his ankle was swollen so badly he could scarcely walk. A tribe of Pawnees south of the Running Water River befriended us, gave us food and ammunition and doctored Roubeau's ankle. We stayed there a week, then cut out across country again on a trail the Pawnees pointed out; that took us to St. Joseph. At St. Joseph, Captain Lowery, a friend of Roubeau's, took us on board his boat, the *Prairie Queen*, and brought us to Sibley. Well," Joel said, rising from his chair and looking at the walnut clock on the mantel, "it is past one o'clock. We had better be on our way to Sibley."

CHAPTER XIV

Pierre Roubeau met them at the door of Cambright's store. "How are you, mademoiselle? And how are the little ones?"

"Very well, thank you, sir."

"And how are you, my fine young friend?" he said, extending his hand to Nat.

For the first time in her life Hannah did not enjoy going into Cambright's store. Mr. Cambright looked up from the ledger he was working on and spoke to them.

Gideon Baxter and two men sitting on barrels came forward to shake hands with Joel.

"Glad to see you back, Joel," Gideon said in his high nasal voice.

Joel looked him straight in the eye, came to the point immediately. "I'm back, Mr. Baxter, but I didn't bring a dollar."

"Yes, that's what Mr. Cambright was telling me. Well, that's too bad."

"You don't know how bad it is," said Joel.

Nat walked to the other end of the store where Ephraim Locke was unpacking carpenters' tools.

Mr. Cambright looked up from his ledger. "Maybe it needn't be as bad as you think, Joel."

"How do you mean?"

Nat came back to stand beside Joel, and Hannah dropped down on a split-bottom chair, her face tense.

"Well, I've watched you young people for a year," Mr. Cambright went on, "and I've made up my mind. I made it up before you came home, Joel, and I have talked it over with your friend, Mr. Roubeau. I have never seen a boy work harder or manage better than Nat. And Hannah has worked right along with him."

"That is certainly true, sir," said Joel.

"Well, your coming back makes it an even better risk, Joel, and your friend, Mr. Roubeau, wants to help. I don't have much money on hand at this time of year but I think my creditors in St. Louis will extend me the cash. You have two hundred and eighty-seven dollars here from the sale of your corn and the hides Nat brought in. I can raise the other four hundred and take up the remainder of the note. You can pay me back as you can in corn, hides and honey. Nat's got a good stand of corn. With enough rain you should have another crop. If you get more land cleared, next year your crop should be bigger."

At that, Nat became all boy. He clapped his heels together, leaped in the air and shouted "Whoopee!"

"You—you mean we can stay on together?" Hannah said, fearing that she had not heard right.

Mr. Cambright nodded and smiled. "Yes, Hannah. I think you have shown yourself to be a good mother to the little family. You deserve to stay together."

Joel, relieved and speechless, found his voice after a moment. "I just don't know what to say, sir. Right now all I can think of is—thank you."

"It's just business, Joel. You boys have proved yourselves. It's a merchant's job to keep farmers in business. Otherwise, I would have no business. You boys have shown that you are a good risk."

"I don't know what I've done," said Joel. "Except save my scalp."

Mr. Cambright chuckled. "Under the circumstances, that was quite a feat. Anyway, you are back to help your family."

"Well, now," said Gideon, "I'm not as mean as you think. You are right, Cambright, about these young people proving themselves. I didn't think they could manage for themselves, but they have, surprisingly. Most surprisingly. You needn't ask your creditors in St. Louis to extend your credit, Cambright. Just put your name on the note and I'll carry it."

"Not at twenty per cent interest."

"Well, now, seeing as how it would be a good safe loan with your name on it, I reckon I could take ten per cent."

"Very well. If I don't have to ask my creditors for a cash advance they can let me have more merchandise. More people are coming out here every month and I would like to carry a bigger stock."

Gideon nodded. "Sound business, Cambright. Sound business."

"Now," said Mr. Cambright, "you boys will need a team of horses. Mr. Roubeau wants to send back two hundred dollars to buy a team to make up in part for the loss of your winter's work, Joel."

"I would like to do more," said Pierre. "But there were those on the trip who lost their lives as well as their goods. Some of them left widows and orphans. I must do for them, too."

"You owe me nothing, Pierre," said Joel. "I went at my own risk, and, after all, I came out better than those who lost their lives. And as you say, there are widows who need your help."

"I insist on doing this much, Joel."

"Then we will accept the money as a loan. We do

145

need the horses, but we shall pay you in corn as soon as the mortgage is paid off."

"No," said Nat. "I will pay him with hides. I had intended sending him some next winter in return for the rifle. I will just keep sending hides until I have paid for the team."

Pierre shrugged and smiled. "Who am I to oppose the convictions of fine young men? That is a bargain, Nat."

Hannah, watching them, was filled with a glow of warm happiness. Nothing gave her greater pleasure than this pride in the upstanding character of the men in her family.

On the way home they took time to stop at Grandma Peabody's to tell her their news. Grandma was overjoyed to see Joel and delighted with their news.

"I knew no Indian would ever get away with your hair, Joel."

Joel gave a short laugh. "They stripped me of about everything but that." Then, to Nat and Hannah, "Well, kids, it looks like it is going to rain. We'd better get home and do up the chores."

"That's right," said Grandma. "Get home and get to work, and pay off that Gideon Baxter. The old scarecrow will never get anything but money out of you now. As long as you work you'll hold that home."

The air was warm and sultry with dark clouds forming in the northwest as they walked back through the woods, but Hannah didn't notice. She was aware of nothing but the song in her heart. Joel was back, they had kept their home, and Joel had promised to go look for little Angie.

They stopped at the Browns' for Jack and Marty; and, although Lizzie pressed them to stay for supper, they declined. They wanted to get their chores done early. Besides, to be at home and together was uppermost in all their minds. Before they got home, the clouds were black and rolling.

"Looks like it is going to be a gullywasher," said Nat.

It was. By the time they reached the cabin, it was coming down in sheets. They were all drenched to the skin before they reached the door. Nat built a fire for Hannah to start supper, then he and Joel went to do the chores.

Hannah heated the leftover ham and greens and turnips and looked about for something extra to add to the meal.

"We have honey in the pot and we've still got a little flour," said Marty. "How about hot biscuits and honey?"

"Just the thing."

The rain was still pelting down when the boys came in from the barn.

"Hot biscuits!" said Joel. "I had almost forgotten there was such a thing."

They had just finished eating when the door opened and Sagameeshee, drenched from head to foot and carrying a bundle under his blanket, came in. The bundle stirred and whimpered. Sagameeshee threw back the blanket, and a head full of tangled reddish curls popped out.

A momentary hush fell over the room, then they were all on their feet at once, shouting.

"It's the baby! It's the baby!"

"Little Angie!"

"Angie! Baby!"

"Precious!"

They surrounded Sagameeshee, all of them reaching for her.

"Give her to me!"

"Give her to me!"

But Sagameeshee put her in Hannah's arms.

Little Angie, startled by the hubbub, puckered her mouth and started to cry. Hannah pressed her to her breast and covered her dirty little face with kisses, crooning softly. Little Angie looked around doubtfully, then, after inspecting each friendly face, she smiled broadly.

"She knows she's home!" Nat shouted. "She knows she's home!"

Sagameeshee sat down by the fire and Nat brought a bowl filled with turnips and ham, then sat down beside him and waited until Sagameeshee was ready to talk.

After each had had a turn at holding little Angie, Hannah wiped off her little hands and face with a damp cloth and sat down at the table to feed her, with Jack and Marty on each side.

"It's almost too wonderful to be true," Hannah sighed.

"Yes, but I feel a little sorry for Mrs. Hopkins, too," said Marty.

Sagameeshee shook his head, grunted. "She got other little one now."

"Really? Then that makes everything right. I'm glad."

When Sagameeshee had finished eating, Joel brought him a pipe filled with tobacco, then took little Angie on his knee while Hannah and Marty washed the dishes. Hannah could hear Sagameeshee talking in low, guttural tones, but she couldn't catch the words.

As soon as the dishes were cleared away, Hannah lighted a candle and took the baby into the bedroom to bathe her. Jack and Marty were right at her heels.

Presently Nat followed them to see little Angie splashing in the washbowl and to tell Hannah what Sagameeshee had said.

"How did he ever do it?" Hannah asked.

"He and his squaw Pokaleeta went down the Osage Trail to the village of the Big Osage in the south part of Missouri. There they learned that the Hopkins had stayed near the Harmony Mission for a time and then had moved on farther south. Sagameeshee and Pokaleeta went on down into the Arkansas Territory to Big Track's tribe near the Three Forks. Big Track sent out scouts and learned that Skip had brought his hides into one of the Chouteau trading posts near Fort Gibson and went with Sagameeshee and Pokaleeta to talk to the colonel. The colonel sent a detachment of men to bring the Hopkins to the fort and made them turn little Angie over to Sagameeshee and Pokaleeta."

"Just imagine their taking all that time and going all those miles!"

"Time and distance mean nothing to an Indian," said Nat. "Especially where friends are concerned."

"Who ever said an Indian isn't smart?" said Hannah.

"Not I," said Nat. "And what is more, he knew to take Pokaleeta along. That colonel would never have turned little Angie over to Sagameeshee without a woman to care for her."

Hannah wrapped a small blanket around little Angie and carried her back to the kitchen.

"Sagameeshee, this is the most wonderful thing in the world that you have done for us," she said, holding little Angie in the firelight to get a better look at her face and shining curls.

"We can't tell you, Sagameeshee," said Joel, "how much this means to us: your spending all this time, traveling all those miles to find our little sister."

"I don't know how we can ever repay you," said Nat.

"You are a friend and a son of a friend," replied Sagameeshee stoically. "You gave corn and meat to feed my little ones. I bring your little one home."

Outside the rain poured and the thunder crashed, but for Hannah, holding little Angie asleep in her arms, all was warmth and cheer inside. Everything seemed perfect with Joel and the baby in the circle around the fireplace. They were all back together now and their house was full of hope.